Isaac P. Hicks

Hicks' Builders' Guide

comprising an easy, practical system of estimating material and labor for

carpenters, contractors and builders - Vol. 3

Isaac P. Hicks

Hicks' Builders' Guide
comprising an easy, practical system of estimating material and labor for carpenters, contractors and builders - Vol. 3

ISBN/EAN: 9783337370725

Printed in Europe, USA, Canada, Australia, Japan

Cover: Foto ©Andreas Hilbeck / pixelio.de

More available books at **www.hansebooks.com**

HICKS'
BUILDERS' GUIDE,

COMPRISING

An Easy, Practical System of Estimating Material
and Labor

FOR

Carpenters, Contractors and Builders.

A COMPREHENSIVE GUIDE TO THOSE ENGAGED
IN THE VARIOUS BRANCHES OF THE
BUILDING TRADES.

By I. P. HICKS.

———

ILLUSTRATED BY NUMEROUS ENGRAVINGS OF ORIGINAL
DRAWINGS.

———

DAVID WILLIAMS, Publisher,
Nos. 96-102 Reade Street, New York.
1893.

PREFACE.

The importance of such a work as "Hicks' Builders' Guide" will be apparent to all making an inspection of its contents, while every one who will give its pages a few hours of careful consideration and attention cannot fail to appreciate the convenience and usefulness of the volume. From actual experience I know there are many things about building which, if arranged for concise and ready reference and put into book form, would be a valuable aid to carpenters, contractors and builders. The frequent inquiries which I have seen in building journals have led me to the belief that a book condensed in form, giving in an easy, practical way general items of interest and value to the trades addressed, is much needed.

this volume it has been the object of the author to point out how mistakes may be avoided in making estimates and to introduce a practical system for making such estimates, thus enabling the carpenter or builder to do the work with greater accuracy. The information in this work has been collected from the close observation and actual experience of a practical workman, who has spent years in the execution of just that class of work with which the majority of workmen meet from day to day.

That the information, methods and rules set forth in this work may serve to instruct and benefit all who become the possessor of a copy of it is the earnest wish of   THE AUTHOR.

OMAHA, NEB., 1893.

POINTS ON ESTIMATING.

To the carpenter and contractor there is nothing of more importance than accurate estimating, for it is one on which success in business largely depends. What is it worth? is a question very frequently asked the carpenter, and he is expected to know at once everything about a building. What is it worth to build a house like Mr. Blank's? What is it worth to build a porch on my house? What is it worth to build a bay window on my house? How much more will it cost to put sliding doors in my house than folding doors? Similar questions by the hundred are daily asked the carpenter, and the persons inquiring naturally expect a prompt answer and a reliable estimate. The question, What is it worth? is often a difficult one to answer, and when applied to a hundred different things it is no wonder the carpenter finds himself beset with difficulties. That thousands of mechanics have long felt the need of some reliable and practical method of estimating material and labor required in building there can be no doubt.

To make an estimate for a building always requires a careful consideration of the plans and specifications, as well as a considerable amount of figuring. Practical experience and personal familiarity with every item that enters into the construction of a building is what every man needs in order to become a good estimator ; yet this is no reason why he cannot learn or profit from the experience of others. In

.his hustling, bustling age of the world the easiest, quickest and surest way of estimating is needed. Such a method can only be acquired by close attention to business, adopting means and methods which will be a safeguard against mistakes and by learning to estimate actual quantities. Before proceeding further with this subject it will be well to explain some of the principal terms used in measuring distances, surfaces and solids.

LINEAR MEASURE.

This is used in measuring distances where length only is considered — without regard to breadth or depth. It is frequently called lineal measure, meaning measured in a line without regard to breadth or depth. It is sometimes called line measure. Fig. 1 shows a lineal foot, drawn to a scale of 1 inch to the foot, the three figures following being to other scales.

Fig. 1.—Lineal Foot.

SQUARE MEASURE.

This is used in measuring surfaces or things whose length and breadth are considered without regard to hight or depth, as sheeting, flooring, plastering, &c.

Fig. 2.—A Square Foot.

Fig. 2 shows a square foot. In the measurement of lumber, square measure is frequently termed board measure, and when used as board measure the thickness is considered as one inch. A square is a figure which has four equal sides, and all its angles right angles, as shown in Fig. 2. Hence a square inch is a square the sides of which are each a lineal inch in length. A square foot is a square the sides of which are each a lineal foot in length, as represented in the diagram. A square yard is a square the sides of which are each a lineal yard in length and contains 9 square feet, as shown in Fig. 3. Square measure is so called because its measuring unit is a square. The standard of square measure is derived from the standard linear measure. Hence a unit of square measure is a square the sides of which are re-

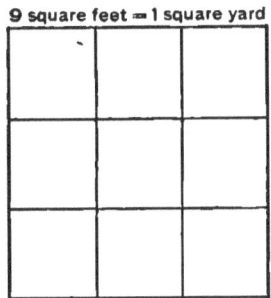

9 square feet = 1 square yard

Fig. 3.—A Square Yard.

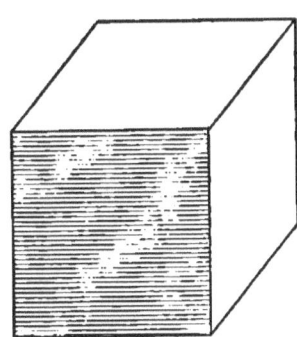

Fig. 4.—A Cubic Foot.

spectively equal in length to the linear unit of the same name.

CUBIC MEASURE.

This is used in measuring solid bodies or things which have length, breadth and thickness, such as stone masonry, the capacity of bins, boxes, rooms, &c. A cube is a solid body bounded by six equal sides. It is often called a hexahedron. Hence, a cubic inch is a cube each of the sides of which is a square inch. A cubic foot is a cube with each of its sides a square foot, as shown in Fig. 4.

Cubic measure is so called because its measuring unit is a cube. The standard of cubic measure is derived from the standard linear measure. A unit of cubic measure therefore is a cube whose sides are respectively equal in length to the linear unit of the same name.

ITEMS AND QUANTITIES.

Having explained the terms used in the measurement of material the next step will be to consider the method of estimating the same. In estimating the lumber required for a building there are many parts for which the amounts required may be listed in a convenient form of table. For example, if we know the amount of material of one kind required for one window frame, we can multiply this amount by the number of frames, and obtain the total amount at once of this kind of material required for frames, and so on with various other parts. Much time will be saved by having a list of this kind, and it will aid very much to insure correctness in estimating. Following is a list of items giving the amount of lumber required for various parts of buildings arranged for concise and ready reference :

LIST OF ITEMS AND QUANTITIES REQUIRED.

	Feet.
Jamb casings for windows, ⅞-inch finish........	10
Jamb casings for windows, 1¼-inch finish........	12
Jamb casings for doors, ⅞-inch finish...........	10
Jamb casings for doors, 1¼-inch finish...........	12
Jamb casings for doors, 1½-inch fiuish...........	15
Jamb casings for doors, 2 -inch finish........ ..	20
Outside casings for windows, ⅞-inch finish......	8
Outside casings for windows, 1¼-inch finish......	10
Outside casings for doors, ⅞-inch finish.........	10
Outside casings for doors, 1¼-inch finish.........	12
Inside window casings, lineal measure...........	20
Inside door casings, one side lineal measure.......16 to	18

Inside door casings, two sides lineal measure......32 to 36
Band molding window frames...................   16
Band molding door frames, one side.............16 to 18
Band molding door frames, two sides ....32 to 36
Molding outside caps of frames...................   4
Sills for windows, per frame, lineal measure......   3½
Sills for doors, per frame, lineal measure......... 4
Window stops, per frame..................... ...12 to 16
Parting stops, per frame...................... ..12 to 16
Door steps, per frame... ....16 to 18
Porch columns, board measure....... ....24 to 30
Brackets, board measure........................ 4 to 6
Horses and treads for stairs, 1¼-inch finish.......90 to 110
For risers and finish about stairs, ⅞-inch finish...30 to 60
Shelving for pantries.........................50 to 100
Shelving common closets.......... .... 4 to 8

PRACTICAL RULES FOR ESTIMATING.

To 3 inch flooring add one-third for the matching.
To 4 inch flooring add one-fourth for the matching.
To 6 inch flooring add one-fifth for the matching.
To 4 inch ceiling add one-third for the matching.
To 6 inch ceiling add one-fifth for the matching.
To 8 inch shiplap add one-sixth for the matching.
To 10 inch shiplap add one-eighth for the matching.
To 12 inch shiplap add one-tenth for the matching.

ESTIMATING SIDING.

To 6-inch beveled siding add one-sixth for the lap
and make no deductions for openings, for in general
the waste in cutting will equal the amount gained
by openings.

ESTIMATING SHEETING.

In estimating sheeting for shingle roofs make no
allowance for spreading the boards. Calculate the
same as for close sheeting a roof, for what is gained
in spreading the boards is generally lost in the cutting. The boards should never be placed more than

2 inches apart for a good roof. Sheeting for gutters on roofs having box cornices is an item often forgotten. These gutters are variously formed, but
usually consist of four pieces of sheeting, forming a
bottom, two sides and a fillet next to the crown molding. The combined width of these pieces is from 1
to 2 feet. Hence the amount of lumber required for
gutters may be found by multiplying the length of
the gutters by the combined width of the pieces
which form it.

For example, suppose the length of gutters on a
building is 42 feet, and to form the bottom, sides and
fillet requires a board equal to $1\frac{1}{2}$ feet wide, how
much lumber will be required ?   Operation : $42 \times 1\frac{1}{2}$
$= 63$ feet.

The sheeting for gutters often amounts to several hundred feet on large jobs, and is a matter worthy of attention. Sheeting is one of the items of
which carpenters usually fall short. The reason is
obvious, it being one of the cheapest kinds of
material. It is used for many purposes for which the
carpenter does not count. Wherever a board is
wanted for one purpose or another, a sheeting board
is taken, provided it will answer, while several hundred feet are usually employed in building scaffolds.
A large portion of this is wasted by being nailed,
sawed and split, It is safe to say that in estimating
sheeting one-fifth should be added to the net estimate.

ESTIMATING SHINGLES.

In estimating shingles allow nine to the square
foot when laid $4\frac{1}{2}$ inches to the weather, and eight
to the square foot when laid 5 inches to the weather.
Common shingles are estimated to average 4 inches

wide, and 250 are put up in a bunch, there being four bunches to the thousand.

Dimension shingles are usually 5 or 6 inches wide, 150 to 180 being put in a bunch, and four bunches counted 1000. In reality there are not 1000 shingles, but being wider than the average of common shingles they are counted the same. There is more waste in laying dimension shingles than the common ones. One-eighth should be allowed for waste in laying dimension shingles.

ESTIMATING STUDDING.

To estimate studding for the outside walls and partitions in houses, estimate them 12 inches from centers, then when they are set the usual distance, 16 inches from centers, there will be enough for all necessary doubling around doors, windows and corners. I prefer this rule for the following reasons : 1. Because it is easier to count the studding 12 inches from centers than 16, as the number of feet in length of an outside wall or a partition gives the number of studding, and is seen at once. 2. Mistakes are less liable than in estimating 16 inches from centers, and adding for double studding, as in adding for double studding more than one-half the places requiring double studding will be overlooked. This rule is not intended to make up for things left out, but is only for making up the number of double studding required around doors, windows and corners. Plates and other places requiring studding must be estimated separately. Studding is another item of which carpenters usually fall short, for the simple reason that many are used in places that were overlooked in the carpenter's estimate. To prove beyond a doubt that the method of estimating 12 inches from centers can be relied upon, we will give a plan, Fig. 5, of the outside walls and partitions of a one-story cottage, and a practical example illustrating the method of estimating.

Referring to the plan, it will be observed that the size is 24 x 32 feet, and that the length of each par-

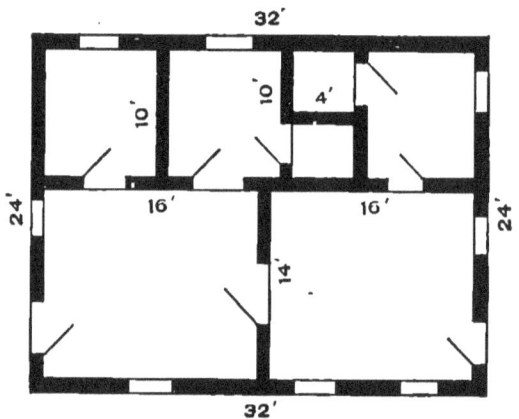

Fig. 5.—Floor Plan of a One Story Cottage, Showing Walls and Partitions.

tition is given. We will suppose it to be a 10-foot story. Now, by the plan it is necessary only to add the length of the outside walls and the partitions together, and to obtain the number of studding required. The operation is as follows:

	Feet.
Two outside walls, 32 feet each	64
Two outside walls, 24 feet each	48
One inside partition	32
One inside partition	14
Three inside partitions, 10 feet each	30
One inside partition	4
Total	192

Thus we see that the total number required is 192 studding.   Now, by the old way of estimating, we would have to find the feet as above.   Multiply by 12, because 12 inches make a foot, and divide the product by 16 inches, the distance the studding are to be placed from centers.   By the old method the work of estimating has but just commenced, but we will help it out a little by an occasional short cut. If we multiply 192 feet by 3 and divide by 4 the result will be the same as though we multiplied by 12 and divided by 16, thus $192 \times 3 \div 4 = 144$ studding, the number required without any doubling. Now comes the work of counting up the places requiring double studding, which is more bothersome than all the rest put together.   In cutting out for the windows the pieces that come out will make the headers ; consequently, if the sides are doubled it will take about three studding to two windows. Now, there are eight windows, which require 12 studding.   This amount can nearly always be saved, as most window frames are made for weights, and the studding has to be set far enough away from the jambs to allow the weights to work freely, and when thus set they seldom require doubling.   In cutting out for the doors the pieces that come out will double one side, and it will require one 10-foot studding to double the other side and make the header.   There are eight doors on the plan, consequently eight 10-foot studding will be required for them.   There are four outside corners, to double which will require four studding.   There are 12 inside partition angles, which we will suppose in this case to require two studding to the corner, which they will not, as one studding has been included in the partition, but we will call it two to the corner, which will make 24 studding. Now, let us sum up and notice the results.

Number of studding estimated 16 inches from centers.... 144
Number of studding for doubling around windows..... 12
Number of studding required for doubling around doors.   8
Number of studding for doubling four outside corners..   4
Number of studding for doubling 12 partition angles..... 24

Total.. 192

Thus, after allowing an abundance for doubling, we still come out even. After all our figuring, the old method has only proven the correctness of the new, and, as it is so much easier than the old, it may meet with favor. As for myself, I can say that I have used the method of estimating studding 12 inches from centers with perfect satisfaction, and have always had a few left. I not only consider it the easiest, but the most accurate way of estimating studding for outside walls and partitions.

At the present day the frame work of most houses is composed principally of studding, such as are used in the outside walls and partitions. This is especially true regarding the plates, rafters and sometimes the ceiling joists. The plates on the outside walls are usually doubled and the partition walls usually have a single plate, top and bottom. The outside walls of small buildings do not require plates across the ends, but on tall buildings it becomes necessary to extend the plates across the ends. To estimate the number of studding required for plates, add together in feet the lengths of the outside walls and partitions which require plates and divide by the length of studding

used for plates.   For example suppose it is required
to put plates all around on the plan shown in Fig. 5,
which is 192 feet, including outside walls and partitions, and that the lengths of studding used is 16
feet ; then 192 ÷ 16 = 12, which represents the number of studding required for a single plate.   This
amount doubled will give the number required for
double plates on the outside walls and single plates
top and bottom, on the partition walls, making 24
studding, the net amount, to which should be added
one-eighth for waste in cutting, making in all 27, the
number required for plates.   If the outside walls and
partitions do not have the same amount of doubling,
or the same number of pieces for plates, then they will
have to be estimated separately.

ESTIMATING FLOOR JOISTS.

These are usually placed 16 inches from centers,
except for floors which are to carry very heavy
weights.   In these the joists are frequently placed 12
inches from centers.   To estimate them 12 inches
from centers add 1 to the number of feet in length
of one wall on which the joists are placed.   For example, suppose a building is 32 feet long, and the
joists are placed 12 inches from centers.   We simply
add 1 to 32, which makes 33, the number of joists
required for one span.   If there are similar spans it
will only be necessary to multiply by the number of
spans.   If the spans are unlike, then estimate each
span separately.   If the joists are placed 16 inches
from centers, then multiply the length of wall by $\frac{3}{4}$
and add 1.   This will give the required number.
Thus if the wall is 32 feet long, then $32 \times \frac{3}{4} + 1 = 25$,
the number required for one span.   The reason for

adding 1 is because the first operation, that of multiplying by ¾, gives the number of spaces between
joists, and one joist more than there are spaces is
always required, except in cases where the sills serve
the place of a joist. In such a case the exact number
will be one less than the number of spaces. A few
extra joists are usually required for doubling and
framing headers around stairways, chimneys, &c. A
little attention given to a plan will show the number
required for this purpose. Ceiling joists, collar
beams and rafters may be estimated in the same
manner.

ESTIMATING CORNICE.

A cornice usually consists of several members, the
most common kind being known as the five-member
cornice, which consists of a planceer, fascia, frieze,
crown and bed molding. To estimate the quantity
of lumber required for a cornice, multiply the length
in feet by the combined width of the planceer,
fascia and frieze in feet. Thus if the planceer is 12
inches wide, the fascia 4 inches and the frieze 12
inches, the combined width is 28 inches, which reduced to feet equals 2⅓. Now, if we have a cornice
120 feet long and 2⅓ feet wide, the operation will be
as follows: 120 × 2⅓ = 280 feet, net amount. In
cutting up lumber for cornice there is always more
or less waste, and it is safe to say that one-eighth
should be added to the net figures. One-eighth of
280 is 35; thus the total amount required is 315 feet
board measure. The bed and crown molding will
each be the same as the length of the cornice, with
one-eighth added for waste in cutting. One-eighth of
120 feet is 15; thus the total amount of molding re-

quired is 135 feet lineal measure. It usually takes a few feet more of the crown molding than of the bed molding on account of the crown molding being on the outside line of the cornice. This difference is hardly worth noticing except on large jobs. The difference usually amounts to from 2 to 3 feet per square turn in the cornice, and is usually estimated by counting the number of turns.

ESTIMATING CORNER CASINGS.

The width of the average corner casing is about 5 inches, and the easiest and quickest way to estimate material for this purpose is to allow 1 foot board measure to each lineal foot in hight per corner. Thus the hight of a corner in feet gives the number of feet board measure required, and is very easy to calculate. For example, if a building has 18 feet studding for outside walls it will require 18 feet of lumber, board measure, per corner for corner casings. Many houses have what are commonly termed belt courses. These are usually casings of the same width as the corner casings and extend around the building at the top or bottom of the window and door frames. To estimate these, find the number of feet, lineal measure, required and divide by 2, which gives the amount in board measure. Board measure is understood to mean 1 inch thick. One quarter must be added for 1¼-inch lumber, and one-half for 1½ inch lumber. In estimating corner casings and belt casings in the manner just described, nothing need be added for waste, because we have estimated the casings 6 inches wide when only 5 inches are required. This allowance is sufficient to cover the waste and makes the computation much easier.

MISTAKES FROM OMISSIONS.

Having given the reader the essential points and short cuts in estimating material, we will now point out what is considerd a source of frequent mistakes, and give a safeguard for it. In estimating material many mistakes are made from omissions. A bill of material for the construction of a building always requires a long list of items, and it frequently happens that some items have been forgotten and left entirely out of consideration. Probably more serious mistakes in estimating material arise from this cause than any other. They are very discouraging to the contractor. They are things he did not count on, but nevertheless he has them to buy, and as extras he always has to pay more for them than he would had he included them in his original bill. Now, if a person had an itemized list of the material entering into the construction of a building, there is no doubt by comparing his bill with the list mistakes from omitting items would be avoided. In a bill there are many items of material that are used for different purposes and different parts of a building, hence to make a list complete in every detail it should mention the part of a building for which each kind of material is used. In the list following, the items which are likely to be used for more than one purpose or part of a building are in full-face type, and the different parts for which the same are likely to be used are in type of the usual face.

LIST OF ITEMS FOR ESTIMATING LUMBER.

Sills.
Side Sills.
End Sills.
Middle Sills.
Trimmers.

Posts.
Main Posts.
Center Posts.
Door Posts.
Basement Posts.

Girts.
Main Girts.
Side Girts.
Tie Girts.

Joists.
First Floor.
Second Floor.
Third Floor.
Ceiling Joists.
Porch Joists.

Studding.
Side Studding.
Gable Studding.
Partition Studding.
Braces.
Plates.
Porches.
Bay Windows.

Roof Timbers.
Common Rafters.
Hip Rafters.
Valley Rafters.
Jack Rafters.
Trusses.
Purlins.
Collar Beams.

Sheeting.
Outside Walls.
Roof Sheeting.
Gutters.
Floor Lining.
Shiplap Sheeting.

Shingles.
Dimension Shingles.

Siding.
Beveled Siding.
Cove Siding.
Barn Siding.

Battens.
⅞ Ogee Battens.
½-inch Battens.
Lattice.

Furring.
1 x 2 Inch.
2 x 2 inch.

Fencing.
4 Inch.
6 Inch.

Paper.
Straw Board.
Tarred Board.

Finish, ⅞ Inch.
Outside Base.
Bay Window Finish.
Porch Finish.
Cornice.
Brackets.
Stair Risers.
Jamb Casings.
Pantry Shelves.
Closet Shelves.

Finish, 1¼ Inch.

Outside Casings.
Corner Boards.
Jamb Casings.
Porch Finish.
Bay Window Finish.
Scroll Work.
Stairs and Steps.
Outside Steps.

Finish, 2 Inch.

Door Sills.
Window Sills.
Jamb Casing.
Brackets.
Cellar Stairs.

Finish, 1⅜ Inch.

Outside Casings.
Outside Steps.

Finish, ½ Inch.

Panels.
Drawer Bottoms.

Flooring.

Main Floors.
Kitchen Floor.
Dining Room Floor.
Porch Floors.

Ceiling.

Porch Ceilings.
Panels.
Wainscoting.
Lining Partitions.

Inside Finish.

Casings.
Corner Blocks.
Plinth Blocks.

Base.
Stair Rail.
Newel Posts.
Balusters.

Molding.

Bed Molding.
Crown Molding.
Panel Molding.
Cove Molding.
Base Molding.
Band Molding.
Quarter Round.
Door Stops.
Window Stops.
Parting Stops.
Wainscoting Cap.
Window Stools.
Water Table.
Thresholds.

Doors.

Front Doors.
Sliding Doors.
Closet Doors.
Cupboard Doors.
Cellar Doors.

Windows.

Bay Windows.
Pantry Windows.
Cellar Windows.
Transoms.
Art Glass.
Plate Glass.

Blinds.

Outside Blinds.
Inside Blinds.

Corner Beads.

GEOMETRICAL MEASUREMENT OF ROOFS.

In the measurement of carpentry work there is probably no part so difficult to master as the accurate measurement of roofs, particularly where they are composed of hips and valleys forming a great variety of irregular surfaces. The shapes of roofs having hips, valleys and gables are usually represented in the form of some triangle. The

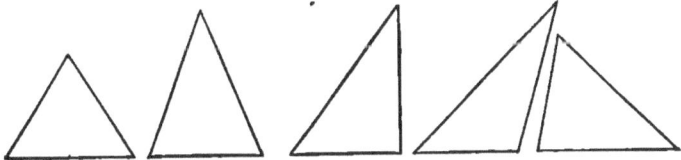

Figs. 6-10.—Different Forms of Triangles.

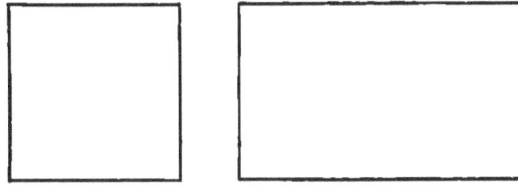

Fig. 11.—A Square.   Fig. 12.—A Rectangle.

different forms of triangles are shown in the diagrams, Fig. 6 representing an equilateral triangle, Fig. 7 an isosceles triangle, Fig. 8 a right-angled triangle, Fig. 9 an obtuse-angled triangle and Fig. 10 a scalene triangle. Figs. 6, 7 and 10 are also acute-angled triangles. Fig. 11 shows a square and Fig. 12 a rectangle. It is a very easy matter to compute the area or surface measurement of a square or a rectangle. The area of a square or a rectangle is

19

found by multiplying its length by its breadth.   In
computing roof measurements all triangles can be
reduced to squares or rectangles of equal areas by
very simple methods.

FINDING THE AREA OF A GABLE.

Referring to Fig. 13, A B C represents the gable
of a building of which A C is the width and D B is
the perpendicular hight.

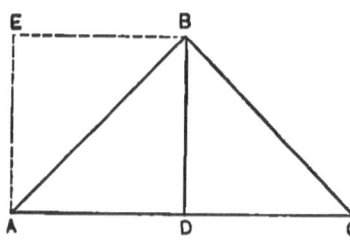

Fig. 13.—Diagram for Finding
Area of a Gable.

By dividing the gable
on the line D B we have
two triangles of equal
areas and equal sides.
It is evident that if the
triangle D B C is
placed in the position
shown by the dotted
lines A E B, it will
form a square whose side is equal to one-half the
width of the gable. This of course applies to gables

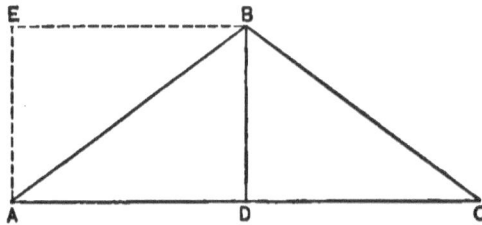

Fig. 14.—Finding Area of Gable when Roof is Less than Half Pitch.

on buildings of a half pitch roof. With a roof of less
pitch a rectangle would be formed with A D for its
length and D B for its breadth, as shown in Fig.
14.   In this figure the triangle A B C is equal in area

to the rectangle Λ E B D. From the foregoing illustrations and principles we derive the following :

Rule.—Multiply one-half the width of the gable by the perpendicular hight.

For example, if a gable is 24 feet wide and the perpendicular hight is 8 feet, then 24 ÷ ½ × 8 = 96 feet, the area of the gable.

FINDING THE AREA OF A TRIANGLE.

Let A B C represent a right-angled triangle, as shown in Fig. 15. If we divide the triangle hori-

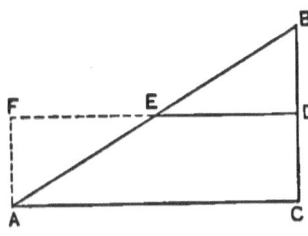

Fig. 15.—Finding Area of a Right-Angled Triangle.

zontally half way on the perpendicular, then the triangle E B D will equal in area the triangle shown by the dotted lines A F E ; hence the triangle A B C equals in area the rectangle A F D C. From the ill ustration we derive the following:

Rule.—Multiply the base by one-half the perpendicular hight.

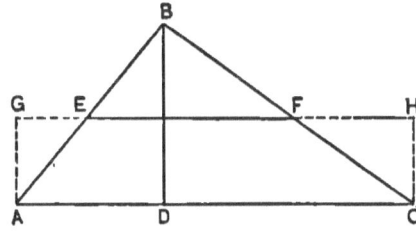

Fig. 16.—Finding Area of a Scalene Triangle.

In Fig. 16 A B C represents a scalene triangle which has no perpendicular line in reality, but for convenience in estimating we draw one, which is

B D, dividing the triangle into two right-angled triangles of unequal areas. By dividing the triangle
horizontally half way on the perpendicular, as shown
by E F, the triangle E B F equals in area the two
triangles shown by dotted lines A G E and F H C.
Hence the triangle A B C equals in area the rectangle
A G H C.

Having shown how triangles may be reduced to
squares and rectangles of equal areas, the next step
will be to show their proper application to roof
measurements.

PLAIN GABLE ROOFS.

The gable roof is the most common in use, and is
formed by two sets of rafters which meet at the
ridge. Fig. 17 shows a plan of
this kind of roof, Fig. 18 a side
elevation, Fig. 19 an end elevation and Fig. 20 showing the size
of roof necessary to cover the
side elevation represented in Fig.
18. An error liable to occur in
taking roof measurements from

Fig. 17.—Plan of Gable Roof.

architectural plans consists in taking the line
A B in the side elevation, Fig 18, for the length

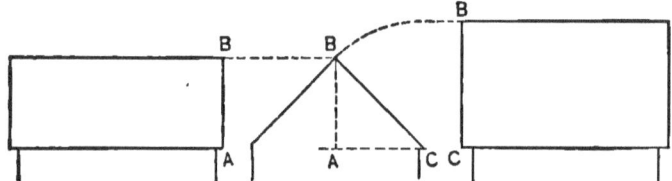

Figs. 18, 19 and 20.—Side and End Elevations of a Gable Roof.

of the rafter. This line is only the perpendicular rise
of the roof, as shown in the end elevation, Fig. 19, by

the dotted line A B. In Fig. 19, B C represents the length of rafter which, when shown in a perpendicular position, is indicated by B C in Fig. 20. This shows the length of roof and of rafter necessary to cover the side elevation, represented in Fig. 18. Hence the area of the roof is found by multiplying the length of the roof by the length of the common rafter, which gives the area of one side. This amount doubled will give the area of both sides.

HIP ROOFS.

The liability to error in estimating the area of hip roofs is still greater than in the case of gable roofs, for no matter from which point we view the eleva-

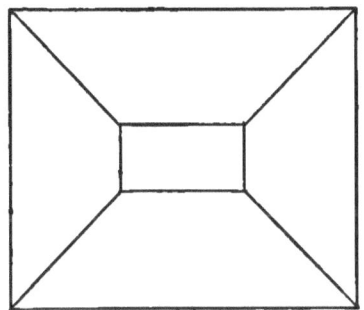
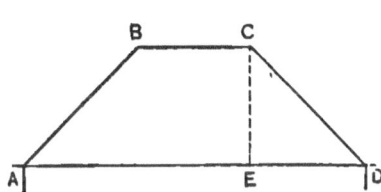

Fig. 21.—Plan of Hip Roof   Fig. 22.—Side Elevation of Roof
with Deck.   shown in Fig. 21.

tions the length of the common rafter is not shown in proper position to indicate the true size of the roof. Fig. 21 shows a plan of a hip roof with deck, and Fig. 22 a side elevation of this kind of roof. In this figure some might take the lines A B and C D for the length of the hips, and C E for the length of the common rafter, but such is not the case. C D shows the length of the common rafter as we would see it on the end looking at the side view, hence E D is the run, E C the rise and C D length of common rafter.   I will now indicate the method of developing the lengths of

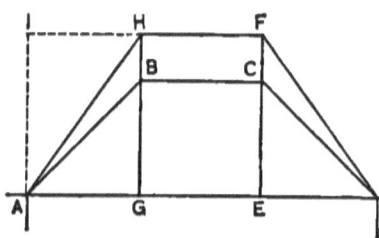

the hips, showing the true size of the roof, and how to reduce the figure to a rectangle of equal area.   Referring to Fig. 23, A B C D and

Fig. 23.—Size and Shape Necessary to Cover Roof.

E represent the same lines as shown in Fig. 22. Now, take the length of the common rafters A B and C D in Fig. 23 and draw them perpendicularly, as shown by E F and G H. Connect F with D and H with A for the length of the hips, then the figure inclosed by the lines A H F D will be the size and shape of the roof necessary to cover the side ele-

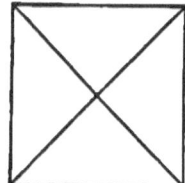
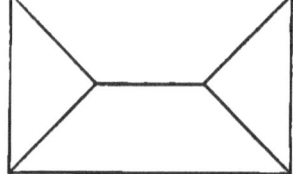

Fig. 24.—Plan of Pyramidal   Fig. 25.—Plan of Roof which
         Roof.   Hips to a Ridge.

vation.   The triangle described by the lines D E F equals in area the triangle A I H, shown by the dotted lines.   Hence the roof A H F D is equal in area to the rectangle A I F E, whose length is one-half the sum of the eaves and deck lengths and whose breadth is the length of the common rafter.   The length multiplied by the breadth gives the area. From the foregoing illustrations and principles we derive the following :

Rule.—Add the lengths at the eaves and deck together, divide by two and multiply by the length of the common rafter. The area of the deck is found by multiplying the length by the breadth.

Example.—What is the area of a hip roof 20 x 28 feet at the eaves, with deck 4 x 8 feet, the length of the common rafter being 10 feet ?

Operation.—20 + 4 + 20 + 4 + 28 + 8 + 28 + 8 ÷ 2 x 10 = 600 feet, the area of the four sides. 4 × 8 = 32 feet, the area of the deck. 600 + 32 = 632, the total area of the roof.

This rule will apply to hip roofs of most any kind. If the roof is pyramidal in form and hips to a point, as shown by Fig. 24, then there is nothing to add for deck, and we simply multiply one-half the length at the eaves by the length of the common rafter. The principles of the three forms of hip roofs are essentially the same.

HIP AND VALLEY ROOFS.

Let Fig. 26 represent the plan of a building having a roof of three gables of equal size and

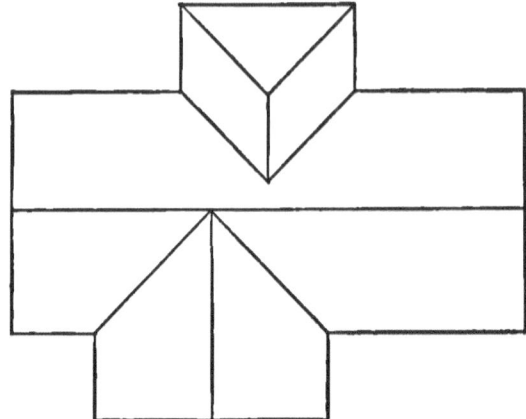

Fig. 26.—Plan of Roof with Four Gables.

one smaller gable hipped on the rear side, as shown in the diagram. Fig. 27 shows this roof as it would appear in the front side elevation. Refer-

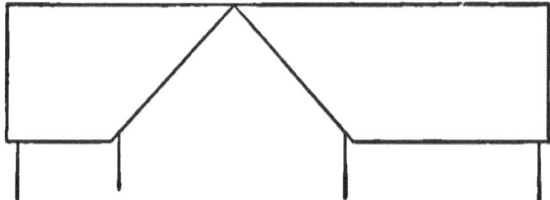

Fig. 27.—Front Elevation of Roof Shown in Fig. 26.

ring now to Fig. 28, A B and B C represent the length of rafters on the front gable. Next set off the length of the common rafters of both the right and left gable perpendicularly, as shown by F G and D E, connecting E with G for the ridge line. On the perpendicular line of the front gable set off the length of the common rafter, shown by the dotted line J H.

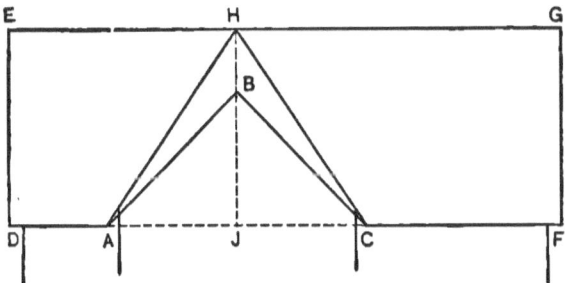

Fig. 2%.—Diagram for Finding Area of Roof Shown in Previous Figure.

Connect H with A and C for the valley rafters, which completes the profile of this side of the roof. The two figures, now represented by A D E H and C F G H, are termed trapezoids. To find the area of a trapezoid multiply half the sum of the parallel sides

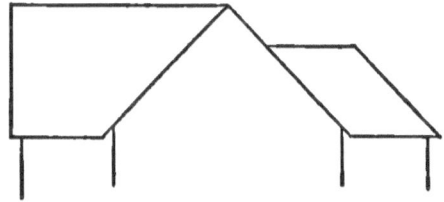

Fig. 29.—Appearance of Roof in Right End Elevation.

by the altitude. In this case to make the matter plain we multiply half the length at the eaves and ridge by the length of the common rafter, which gives the area of the roof necessary to cover the elevation shown in Fig. 27.

Fig. 29 shows the roof as it would appear in the right end elevation. We will now develop the

shape of the roof and obtain the necessary lengths
for finding the area of this elevation. Referring
now to Fig. 30, A B and B C represent the length of
rafters on the right gable. Next set off the length of
rafter on the front gable shown by D E. Then set off
the same length in the center of the left gable shown
by the dotted line J H. Connect H with E for ridge
line of front gable. Connect H with A and C for the
valley rafters. Now take half the width of the rear
gable, which is to be hipped on the end, and in this

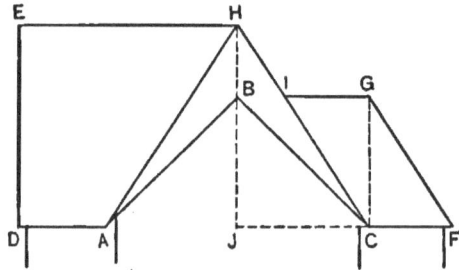

Fig. 30.—Diagram for Finding Area of Roof Shown in Fig. 29.

case is represented by C F   From C erect a perpendicular the length of the common rafter on this part,
shown by the dotted line C G. Connect G with F
for the hip rafter and draw the ridge line G I parallel with C F, which completes the profile of this
view of the roof. The figure shown by A D E H is
a trapezoid, and its area may be found as has been
previously described for such figures. The figure
shown by C F G I is termed a rhomboid. Its area
may be found by multiplying C F by C G, or, in
other words, the length at the eaves multiplied by
the length of the common rafter gives the area.
The areas of the two figures added completes the
area of the roof necessary to cover the end elevation

shown in Fig. 29. As the left end elevation is similar to the right in shape and size the last estimated area doubled will give the area of the roof necessary to cover the two end elevations.

We have now to consider the rear elevation and the roof necessary to cover it. Fig. 31 shows the roof as it

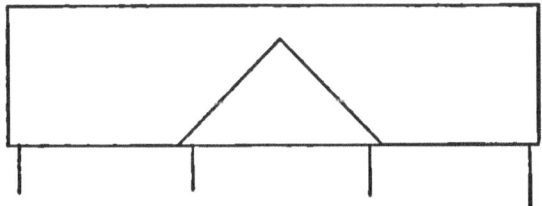

Fig. 31.—Roof as it Appears in Rear Elevation.

would appear in the rear elevation. We will now develop the shape of the roof and obtain the necessary lengths and lines for finding the area of this elevation. Referring to Fig. 32, A B and B C represent the length of the common rafters on the rear gable.

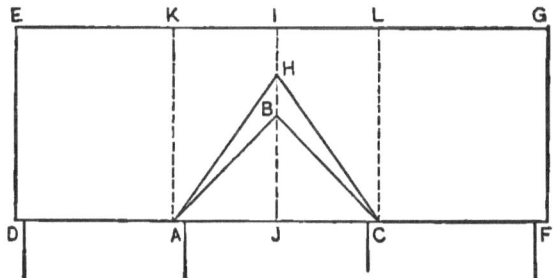

Fig. 32.—Diagram for Finding the Area of Roof Shown in Fig. 31.

From the center of the gable set off the length of the common rafter, as shown by the dotted line J H. Connect H with A and C for the length of the hips. Set off the length of the common rafter on the right and left gable, as shown by F G and D E ; connect E and

G for the ridge line, which completes the profile of the rear view of the roof. It will be seen that the ridge of the rear gable does not come up even with the ridge of the other two ; hence the rear elevation shows a different shape than the front. For conven·ience in estimating, we divide the roof in the center of the gable, shown by the dotted line H I; then divide the roof perpendicularly each side of the gable, as shown by the dotted lines A K and C L. We now have the roof divided into four figures, of which D E K A and C L G F are rectangles, A K I H and C L I H are trapezoids. As the method of obtaining the areas of such figures has been previously described, further explanation is unnecessary. It has now been shown how to find the area of each side of the roof, as indicated in the plan, Fig. 26. By adding the area of the four sides the total area of the roof will be obtained.

THE CIRCLE.

A circle, Fig. 33, is a plane figure bounded by one uniformly curved line called the circumference. The

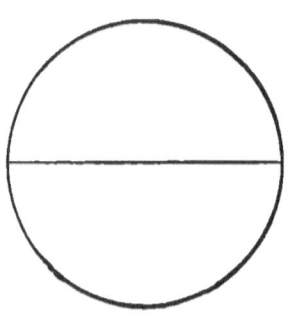

diameter of a circle is a straight line drawn through the center and terminating at the circum· ference. The radius is a straight line drawn from the center to the circumference, and is there- fore half the diameter.

To find the circumference of a circle from its diameter, multi- ply the diameter by 3.14159.

Fig. 33.—A Circle.

To find the diameter of a circle from its circumfer- ence, divide the circumference by 3.14159.

To find the area of a circle multiply half the circumference by half the diameter, or multiply the square of the diameter by the decimal .7854.

To find the side of the greatest square that can be inscribed in a circle of a given diameter, divide the square of the given diameter by 2 and extract the square root of the quotient.

TO FIND THE RADIUS OF A CIRCLE FROM A SEGMENT.

Let A C, of Fig. 34, represent the chord of an arc. From the center of A C square up the rise of the segment to B. Connect B with A and C. From the

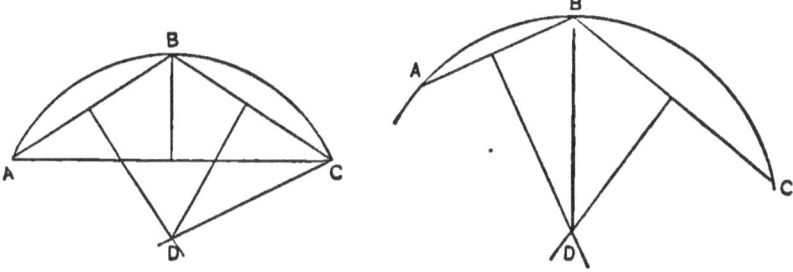

Fig. 34.—Diagram for Finding Radius   Fig. 35.—Drawing a Circle
from a Segment.   Through Three Points.

center of A B and B C square down the lines as shown. The point of crossing at D is the center of the circle, and D C is the radius.

TO DRAW A CIRCLE THROUGH THREE POINTS.

Set off any three points, as A B C, Fig. 35, Connect A B and B C by straight lines. From the center of A B and B C square down to D, as shown, which will be the center of the circle. D B is therefore the radius of the circle which will strike the three points A B C.

POLYGONS.

A plane figure bounded by more than four lines is called a polygon. It must therefore have at least five sides, and the number of sides which it may have is not limited. In this work will be introduced only the forms in common use, for the purpose of showing simple methods of estimating their areas

A regular polygon has all its sides and angles equal, as shown in Fig. 36. An irregular polygon has its sides and angles unequal, as shown in Fig. 37.

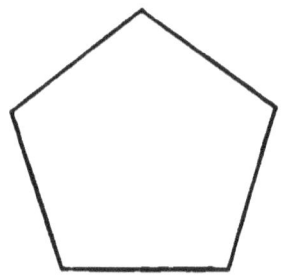

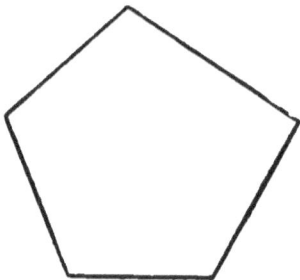

Fig. 36.—A Regular   Fig. 37.—An Irregular
        Polygon.   Polygon.

A polygon of five sides, as shown in Fig. 36 or 37, is called a pentagon. The diagonal is a straight line drawn between any two angular points of a polygon. The diameter is a straight line drawn from any angle through the center to the opposite side or angle, as the case may be.

To find the area of a regular pentagon we will let A B C D E represent the sides of a regular pentagon, as shown in Fig. 38. Draw the diameter A F and connect E with B, which divides the pentagon into four figures—namely, two right angled triangles of equal areas and two trapezoids of equal areas. E G

multiplied by G A will give the area of the two triangles. Half the sum of D C and E B multiplied by
G F will give the area of the two trapezoids. The
two areas added will give the total area.

To find the area of an irregular pentagon, we will
let A B C D E represent the sides, as shown in Fig. 39.
Next draw A D and A C, which will divide the pentagon into three triangles of unequal areas; then
draw the altitude of these triangles, which is the per-

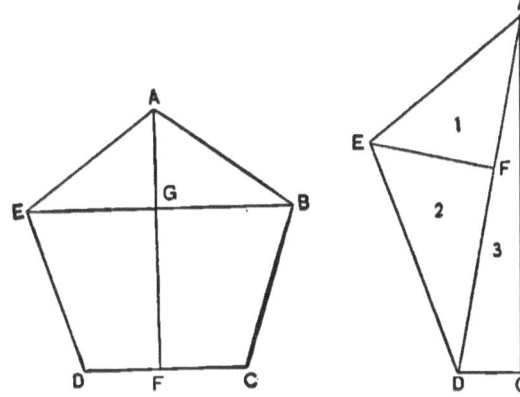 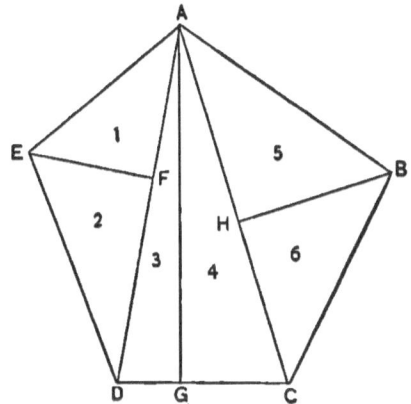

Fig. 38.—Finding Area of   Fig. 39.—Finding Area of an
    Regular Pentagon.   Irregular Pentagon.

pendicular distance from their vertices to the opposite sides, called the base and shown by the lines E F,
A G and B H. This divides the figure into six right
angled triangles of unequal areas. A D multiplied by
half the altitude E F will give the area of triangles
1 and 2, or A E D ; then D C multiplied by half the
altitude A G will give the area of triangles 3 and 4,
or D A C. Again A C multiplied by half the altitude
H B will give the area of triangles 5 and 6, or A B C.
The three areas added will give the total area.

A polygon of six sides is called a hexagon, and is shown in Fig. 40. To find the area of this figure draw the diagonals as shown in Fig. 41, which divide the hexagon into equal triangles, the size of

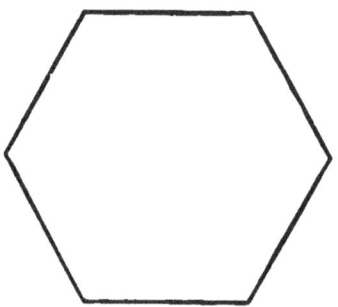

Fig. 40.—A Hexagon.   Fig. 41.—Finding the Area
                                    of a Hexagon.

which is represented by A B C. Next draw the altitude of this triangle, as shown by the dotted line B D. Now, A C multiplied by half the altitude B D

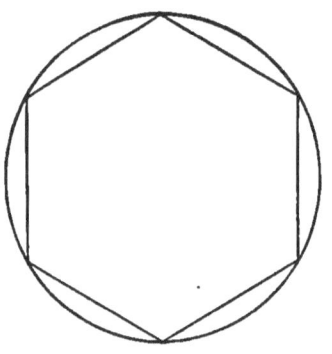
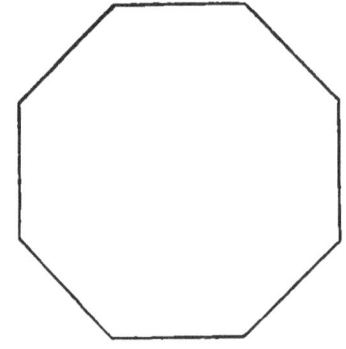

Fig. 42.—Describing any Reg-   Fig. 43.—An Octagon.
ular Polygon.

will give the area of the triangle A B C, and this multiplied by six will give the total area. The area of
any regular polygon may be found by drawing lines

from all of its angles to the center, thus forming triangles of equal areas, w'·ich may be estimated by
multiplying the base by one-half the altitude, as
shown in Fig. 41. To describe any regular polygon
draw the circumference of a circle; divide the circumference into as many equal spaces as the polygon has
sides, connect these points with straight lines, and
the polygon is completed, as shown in Fig. 42.

A polygon of eight sides is called an .octagon and
is shown in Fig. 43. In Fig. 44 is represented a plan

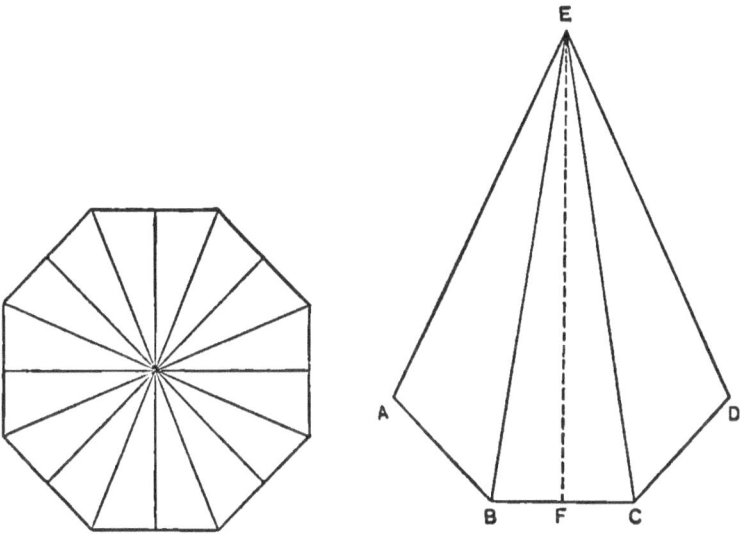

Fig. 44.—Plan of an Octagon   Fig. 45.—An Elevation of an
        Tower Roof.   Octagon Tower Roof.

and in Fig. 45 an elevation of an octagon tower roof.
In Fig. 45 A B C D represent the plates and A E,
B E, C E and D E the hip rafters. The dotted line
F E represents the common rafter. To find the area
of this roof multiply B C by half of F E and this

product by eight, the number of sides. It will now be seen that the area of any tower roof from a square to a polygon of any number of sides may be found by multiplying the length of its side by half the length of the common rafter. If the tower has a round base then the circumference of its base multiplied by half the length of the common rafter will give the area. The reader has now been shown wherein it is possible to make mistakes in the measurement of roofs, as indicated by the elevations. It has been shown how to develop the true shapes and sizes of irregular roof surfaces and how to reduce them to squares or rectangles of equal areas, or to figures whose areas are· easily calculated. I might go on illustrating and describing roofs seemingly without end, but enough has been illustrated to thoroughly show the principles and methods of estimating roof surfaces. By a little study of the principles and methods, as previously set forth, the reader will be able to make proper application· of them to the surface measurement of any roof.

It will be noticed in nearly all cases that the essential measurements for computing the area or surfaces of roofs are—1, the length at the eaves ; 2, the length at the ridge or deck, as the case may be, and 3, the length of the common rafter.

In works of this kind it has been customary to show a number of illustrations on geometry, merely indicating how to construct certain figures from a given side or a few given points, while in all cases the most important part which a carpenter requires— that of computing the area of irregular surfaces—has been omitted. In the art of carpentry there is no place in which these irregular-shaped figures appear as frequently as they do in the construction of roofs, and if the carpenter has no accurate methods for computing their areas then he has to make a guess, which is the course taken by many who have never seen a proper application of geometry to the surface measurement of roofs. Roof surfaces have to be estimated in order to ascertain the amount of material required to cover them, as the sheeting, shingles, slate, tin, copper, iron, &c., or whatever may be used for the roof covering. In the illustrations and examples given there might have been presented many rules for finding the length of certain sides of a figure, by having the lengths of one or more of the other sides, but they would be merely mathematical problems, which in most cases could be solved only by square root. As many carpenters. are not conversant with square root it has been deemed best to avoid its use as much as possible in this work, and especially in places where it is not needed. It must be generally conceded in taking roof measurements, that if a carpenter can measure one distance he can measure the roof to find any distance he may desire to know. Therefore the illustrations given have been more to show how to measure roofs to obtain the proper dimensions for computing their areas than as geometrical problems and methods of construction. The author has considered the subject of roof measurement worthy a place by itself in estimating, and the subject of roof framing will be taken up, thoroughly illustrated and described in another part of this work.

ESTIMATING LABOR FOR CARPENTRY WORK.

It is generally claimed that the question of labor is the most difficult and uncertain the carpenter is called upon to solve. Material can often be figured very closely, but just how long it will take to work up a lot of material and place it in position in a building can not be so easily determined. The cost of labor depends upon the time required to perform a certain amount of it. All men do not work alike; some will do easily one-third more than others—hence the time required to perform a certain amount of labor depends largely upon the ability of the men employed, the advantages they take in doing work and the skill of the foreman in the management as it progresses day by day. It is an easy matter to find four men who will do as much in a day as five others, and to illustrate the surprising result of the difference in the ability of men to perform labor, I will give a practical example.

Suppose two contractors, A and B, each have a job of work exactly the same. A takes his job for $900 and B his for $800. Each pays wages at the rate of $2.50 per day, and each employs five men; but four of B's men are equal to five of A's and it takes 60 days to complete his job. Which will make the most money, and how much? The solution of this problem is as follows: If A employs five men at $2.50 per day for 60 days, the labor will cost him $750; as he took his job for $900, his profit is $150. Now if four of B's men are equal to five of A's, B will

complete his job in one-fifth less time than A, which
will be 48 days. Now, if B employs five men at $2.50
per day for 48 days, the labor will cost him $600, and,
as he took his job for $800, his profit is $200. Thus we
can see how one man can underbid his competitor
$100 on $900 worth of work and still make the most
money. Again, suppose it required B 52 days to
complete his job ; even then he could bid $100 lower
than A and still make as much money. The above
example shows at least one chance for the surprising
difference in builders' estimates on the same work.
It also shows how the difference in the ability of the
workmen employed and the management of the work
can make a vast difference in the cost of a building.
Under such circumstances how can a contractor
make estimates upon which he can rely ?

In all kinds of work there must be an average,
and this average is what is wanted as a standard in
estimating. If labor cannot be estimated from what
is known to be an average day's work, then we
naturally conclude it must be estimated by com-
parison or guessed at. The best way for a contractor
to obtain facts and figures that he can rely upon in
estimating is to keep a record of all the work he does.
It will not do to trust to memory, for in a few months
or a year he will not know whether such and such
work cost $42 or $54, or what it cost. If he would
profit by experience he will keep a record of the cost
of his work, so that he can refer to it at a moment's
notice. To keep a record that will give the best
and most reliable facts and figures prepare a list of
all kinds of work, having two sets of money columns,
one for estimated cost and one for actual cost.

When estimating a job put down the estimated cost, and when the actual cost is found from experience in doing the work put it down, and keep each particular kind of work or portions of a job separate from the entire job. By so doing one will soon be able to see where he has estimated too high or too low, and will have facts and figures which will enable him to make a proper average. Some parts of a building are easily estimated by the "square," which contains 100 square feet. Some parts are easily estimated by the lineal foot, while other portions are best estimated by the piece. Keep a record of the time required by different men in doing work by the square, lineal foot or piece. In this way one will find the average day's work from actual experience, which is the only plan that can be followed with success.

When it is known what it is worth to do work by the square, lineal foot or piece, any person of ordinary skill in figuring ought to be capable of making an estimate reasonably accurate. As I have said before, the average day's work of all kinds is what is wanted as a standard in estimating. Accordingly I have prepared a table with the average day's work of each kind and the average rates to figure on. The table is made on a basis of ten hours for a day's work and as near as practical to average $3.50 per day. If an estimate is wanted for nine hours add one-tenth to the price ; and if for eight hours add one-fifth. The prices can easily be made for any rate per hour or any number of hours per day. To those who want to test the advantage of a table of this kind I would say, do not take it for granted that my rates and averages are the best in the world, or that they are just the thing for a guide, but prepare a similar list and begin entering rates and averages as they are found from actual experience. Then one will have something that will suit the locality in which he lives, and there can be no doubt that in a short time he will have something that will be much to his advantage in estimating. Let me say however, that the average day's work as found in the table is a reasonable average, as I have found from experience, and considerable dependence can be placed on estimates made from it.

POINTS ON ESTIMATING LABOR.

While the tables show the average day's work with the average rate per square, per lineal foot, and per piece for nearly all kinds of carpentry work, yet I

TABLE OF PRICES FOR ESTIMATING LABOR BY THE LINEAL FOOT.

Different kinds of work per lineal foot.	Average day's work. No. of feet.	Rate per foot.
Putting down base and quarter round	90	$0.04
Putting on base molding	180	.02
Cap and molding for wainscoting.......	140	.02½
Putting up cornice....................	24	.15
Making gutters in cornices............	50	.07
Putting up corner casings	70	.05
Putting on belt casings...............	90	.04

think it proper to show how and why variations should sometimes be made, and that it is necessary to use some discriminating judgment in connection with the tables as regard the average day's work. Undoubtedly, many will think the rates in the table too high, and the averages too low, but right here

TABLE OF PRICES FOR ESTIMATING LABOR BY THE SQUARE.

Different kinds of work per square.	Average day's work. No. of squares.	Rate per square.
Framing floors in houses............ ..	5	$0.70
Framing floors in barns..............	4	.90
Framing outside walls of houses	6	.60
Framing outside walls of barns........	4	.90
Framing and setting partitions........	6	.60
Framing ceilings....................	7	.50
Framing plain roofs.............. .	6	.60
Framing hip and valley roofs........ .	3	1.20
Sheeting sides with com non sheeting...	8	.45
Sheeting sides with 8-inch shiplap.....	7	.50
Sheeting sides with 6-inch flooring......	6	.60
Sheeting roofs with common sheeting...	8	.45
Sheeting roofs with 8-inch shiplap.....	6	.60
Shingling with common shingles.......	2½	1.40
Shingling with dimension shingles.....	2	1.75
Siding with 6-inch beveled siding......	3	1.20
If papered before siding..........	2½	1.40
Siding with 6-inch cove siding........	2½	1.40
If papered before siding....	2	1.75
Siding with 12-inch barn boards.......	6	.60
Siding with 12-inch boards and battened	4	.90
Laying floor with 6-inch pine flooring..	6	.60
Laying floor with 4-inch pine flooring..	4½	.80
Laying floor with 6-inch hardwood....	5	.70
Laying floor with 4-inch hardwood....	4	.90
Laying floor which has to be surfaced..	2	1.75
Ceiling with 6-inch pine ceiling.......	4	.90
Ceiling with 4-inch pine ceiling...	3	1.20
Plain wainscoting without cap........	4	.90

let me say that no contractor should make an estimate based on these so-called big day's work. If he does he is almost sure to find he is mistaken. An estimate should always be made from a reasonable average, and then if the contractor is able to average as well as he estimates, and perhaps a little better, he feels that he is making a success of his business

TABLE OF PRICES FOR ESTIMATING LABOR BY THE PIECE.

Different kinds of work per piece.	Average day's work. No. of pieces.	Rate per piece.
Making plain window frames	3	$1.20
Making plain door frames......	4	.90
Making transom frames	3	1.20
Setting frames in position in building.	14	.25
Hanging blinds before frames are set.	15	.24
Hanging blinds after frames are set....	10	.35
Hanging inside blinds.................	5	.70
Fitting sash in frames.............. .	18	.20
Hanging sash with weights	14	.25
Hanging transoms....................	10	.35
Casing windows	12	.30
Casing doors, one side......	16	.22
Casing doors, both sides	8	.44
Casing transom frames, one side.......	12	.30
Casing transom frames, both sides......	6	.60
Cutting in window stops.............	35	.10
Cutting in door stops................	30	.12
Band molding frames, one side.........	24	.15
Band molding frames, two sides........	12	.30
Putting down thresholds	24	.15
Fitting common doors................	20	.18
Hanging common doors..............	20	.18
Putting on rim knob locks	35	.10
Putting on mortice knob locks.........	14	.25

and is satisfied. On the other hand, if the estimate is made from too large an average, the big day's work which was counted on may not be accomplished and many a time, what seemed like time enough, would prove insufficient.   Then there would be dissatisfaction and disappointment.   I will now return to the tables and show how to make some short cuts by combinations.   In the tables every item is given separately for convenience in estimating any particular portion of a job, but to facilitate the work of estimating an entire job, many of the different items may be combined and regarded as one.   For example, it is worth—

For framing and placing joists in position per

square...$0.70 to $0.90

Laying floor per square........................ .60 to 1.75

Total ....$1.30 to $2.65

Thus the framing and laying of floors may be estimated at once if desired.   The bridging of joists should be estimated at 3 to 5 cents per joist for each row of bridging.

DOUBLE FLOORS.

Where one floor is laid over another it is worth one-fourth more to lay the second floor than the first. Thus if it is worth 60 cents per square to lay the first floor, it is worth 75 cents per square to lay the second, or $1.35 per square for both.   Framing floors for brick buildings may be estimated at the same rate as for frame, for, while there is usually less framing, more time is required to place joists in position and level up, thus making the labor about equal.   As a building progresses in hight more time is required to place joists in position, hence 10 per cent. should be added to each succeeding story after the first. The outside walls of a house may be estimated as follows:

To frame and raise, per square	$0.60 to $0.90
Sheeting the same, per square.	.45 to .60
Siding the same, per square.	1.20 to 1.75
Total.	$2.25 to $3.25

Thus the outside walls of a house may be estimated at $2.25 to $3.25 per square.

Framing should include raising and sheeting ; and siding should be estimated sufficiently high to cover the cost of building scaffolds. It is worth one-third more to sheet a building inside than outside, and twice as much to sheet it diagonally. The siding of a house is subject to large variations, as a man can often side three or four times faster on some buildings than he can on others. The amount an average workman will put on in a day depends upon the number, size and shape of the openings around which he has to side, the hight of the building and the amount of scaffolding he has to do. Difficult places to side can be readily seen on a building or even from a plan, and the siding should be estimated sufficiently high to cover the cost. I have known men to put on siding for 60 cents per square, but not one man in ten can make anything like respectable wages at this price, even on the plainest kind of work and under the most favorable circumstances. Some men may be able to put on four squares a day and perhaps a little more than that, but the large majority will fall short of four, and some will not put on more than two squares a day. The average is therefore not more than three squares per day, which would amount to $1.80 per day, with chances of not doing so well. In estimating siding or sheeting by the square no deduction is made for openings. Roofs may be estimated as follows :

For framing, per square........................ .. $0 60 to $1.20
For sheeting. per square.................... . .45 to .70
For shingling, per square....................... 1.25 to 1.75

Total....................................$2.30 to $3.65

Thus to frame, sheet and shingle a roof it is worth from $2.30 to $3.65 per square. Each hip or valley in a roof is worth from 75 cents to $1.50 for sheeting and shingling. Hips and valleys cannot be shingled or sheeted with as much speed as plain roofs, and are seldom estimated high enough. The shingling of belt courses and gables with dimension shingles is worth from $2 to $3.50 per square, according to the windows and difficult places with which the workman has to contend.

CORNICES.

A cornice is composed of several members, the most common kind containing five, which are known respectively as planceer, fascia, frieze, crown and bed moldings. It may be estimated at 15 cents per lineal foot. If a cornice has more than five members add 2 to 3 cents per lineal foot for each member. If there are less than five members a similar deduction may be made. If a cornice has brackets it will be necessary to add a sufficient amount to cover the cost of putting them up.

GUTTERS.

These are variously formed on roofs and in cornices and are worth from 4 to 10 cents per lineal foot. A standing gutter on a roof is worth from 4 to 6 cents per foot. A flush gutter or one sunk in a roof or cornice is worth from 6 to 10 cents per foot. Fig. 46 shows a cornice with a standing gutter on the roof. The gutter is usually placed on the second or third course of shingles, and consists of one piece standing square with the roof, as shown by the dotted lines, and is usually supported by small brackets on the

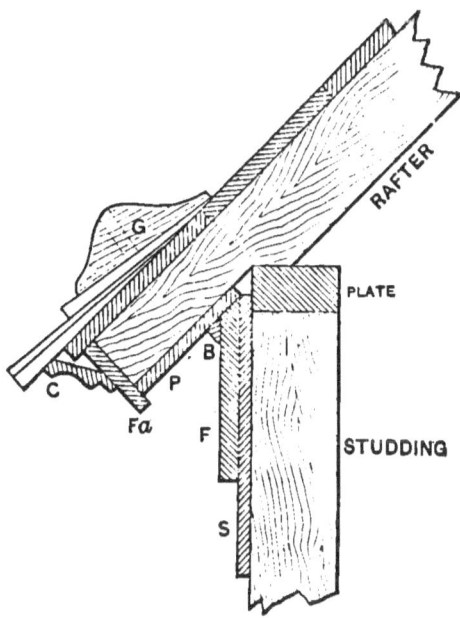

Fig. 46.—Cornice with Standing Gutter.

under side with end pieces as shown. G is the gutter, C the crown molding, F*a* the fascia, P the planceer, B the bed molding, F the frieze and S the sheeting. Fig. 47 shows a gutter formed in the cornice with four pieces—namely, a bottom, two sides and a fillet, all as shown by the dotted lines. G is the gutter, FL the fillet, C the crown mold, F*a* the

fascia, P the planceer, B the bed molding, F the
frieze and S the sheeting. To make this kind of a
gutter is worth 10 cents per lineal foot.

PORCHES.

Sometimes porches may be estimated by the lineal
foot, at from $2 to $4 per foot. This, however, is not

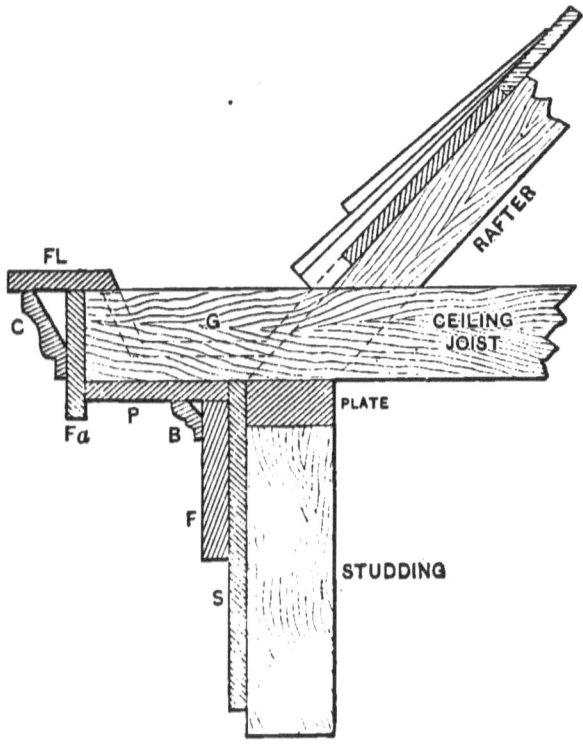

Fig. 47.—Gutter Formed in the Cornice.

the best method, its principal advantage being its
simplicity and ease. The most common kind of
porches, with which almost every one becomes familiar, may be estimated as above with generally satisfactory results. The best and most accurate way,

however, is to estimate the framework, flooring, ceiling and roofing by the square; the cornice, gutters and latticework by the foot, and the steps, columns, brackets and ornamental work by the piece. After summing up the various parts the result may be taken as the most reliable estimate.

ESTIMATING WINDOW FRAMES.

The various parts of the work necessary to complete a window frame in a building may be put down as follows :

Making frame..	$1.25
Hanging blinds..	.25
Setting frame in building....................................	.25
Fitting sash...	.20
Hanging sash with weights..................................	.20
Casing window...	.30
Band molding frame	.12
Cutting in stops...	.09
Total..	$2.66

Thus we see that plain window frames complete in a building, may be estimated at $2.66 each. It should be remembered that a fine hardwood finish is often worth twice or three times as much as a common soft wood finish, and that large transom frames, twin windows, &c., finished in hardwood may be worth as high as $20.

DOOR FRAMES.

The different parts of work required to complete a door frame may be estimated as follows :

Making frame....... ....$0.90
Setting frame in building .... .25
Casing frame.......... .... .44
Band molding frame .... .24
Fitting and hanging door... .... .86
Putting on mortice lock........................ .. .... .25
Cutting in thresholds.......... .... .15
Cutting in stops .... .12

    Total $2.71

Thus it is worth $2.71 per frame to make and finish common door frames complete in a building. By looking over the above estimate it will be seen that there is a great deal of work about a door frame besides fitting and hanging the door and putting on the lock—hence many are apt to estimate too low. To fit, hang and put a lock on a common door, using one pair of loose pin butts and a common mortice lock, is worth 60 cents. The average day's work is about six doors per day. If the doors are large and require three butts each, it is worth 75 cents per door. Front doors having complicated locks with night keys, &c., are worth $1.50 to $2 per door.

SLIDING DOORS.

The different parts of work required to put up sliding doors are worth as follows :

Lining partitions and putting up track............. .... $7.00
Setting jambs.................................. ..... 1.00
Casing door frame.... .... 1.00
Band molding frame................................ . .30
Hanging doors and putting on lock................... 8.50
Cutting in stops... .... .20

    Total $13.00

Thus sliding doors are worth $13 per set, and may vary according to size and style of finish up to $30.

A single sliding door is worth very nearly as much as double doors. The difference in the labor of putting them up in most cases would not be over $2.

FOLDING DOORS.

The cost of labor for putting in folding doors complete is from $3.75 to $5.50 per set. To fit, hang and put on lock and flush bolts is worth from $1.75 to $3.50 per set.

WAINSCOTING.

Plain wainscoting is worth about 90 cents per square. The cap should be estimated by the foot extra, according to style of finish. Paneled wainscoating is often worth twice or three times as much as plain work.

SINKS.

To finish a kitchen sink in the plainest style is worth $2, and some styles finished in hardwood are worth as much as $10.

BATHROOMS.

A bathroom having in connection a wash bowl and a water closet, finished in the plainest style, will take a good workman two days, and is worth $7. An inexperienced hand in this kind of work will require about three days to complete the job. Some styles of hardwood finish will require from four to six days' work and are worth from $14 to $21.

PANTRIES.

The shelving and finishing of a pantry in the plainest style is worth from $3 to $5. Pantries with flour chests, spice drawers and numerous other things, shelves inclosed with doors, all elegantly fitted up, are worth from $25 to $40.

STAIRS.

The cheapest kind of cellar stairs are worth from $3 to $5, and the plainest kind of box stairs from $8 to $12 per flight. Plain open stairs with hand rail, newel post and balusters are worth from $20 to $35. Stairs and staircases finished in hardwood may vary from $50 to $150. It is frequently worth from $10 to $20 to set the newel posts and put up the rail of some of the most elaborate designs.

RECAPITULATION.

In looking over the items which have been variously combined and bringing them to a minimum, it will be seen on what the carpenter has to figure and the easiest way of estimating it.

Framing and laying floors, per square	$1.30 @	$2.65
Framing, sheeting and siding, per square	2.25 @	3.25
Framing and setting partitions, per square	.60 @	.90
Framing, sheeting and shingling roofs, per square	2.30 @	3.65
Hips and valleys, each	.75 @	1.50
Shingling belt courses and gables, per square.	2.00 @	3.50
Cornice, per lineal foot	.10 @	.15
Corner casings, per lineal foot	.04 @	.06
Gutters, per lineal foot	.06 @	.10
Porches, per lineal foot	2.00 @	4.00
Window frames, complete, in building, each.	2.60 @	20.00
Door frames, complete, in building, each	2.70 @	20.00
Sliding doors, complete, in building.	13.00 @	30.00
Folding doors, complete, in building	3.75 @	5.50
Wainscoting, per square	.90 @	2.70
Wainscoting cap, per lineal foot	.02 @	.05
Sinks, each	2.00 @	10.00
Bathrooms, finished complete	7.00 @	21.00
Putting down base in houses, per lineal foot..	.03 @	.05
Finishing pantries	3.00 @	40.00
Cellar stairs, very common	3.00 @	5.00
Plain stairs	20.00 @	35.00
Front stairs	30.00 @	150.00

SHORT CUT IN ESTIMATING.

As many of the principal parts of construction in common buildings are essentially the same, a short cut may be made in figuring the bulk of the rough work, which includes the framing, raising, sheeting, siding, roofing, laying of floors, and setting partitions. Take the number of cubic feet in the building from top of foundation to top of ridge of roof and multiply by the rate per cubic foot, which is usually from two to three cents. After estimating the rough work in this manner add all the parts that are considered of a changeable character, such as the cornice, gable trimmings, porches, bay windows, inside finish, and all parts not included in the bulk of the estimates. Of course one can see that a change in price will change the amount of the estimate, and that it is as necessary to use discriminating judgment in fixing rates for this method as in any other.

To successfully estimate the labor in a building every one must fix his own rates from personal experience in doing the class of work which he is called on to perform. Tables, prices and methods are good in their way, and many times will give valuable aid in estimating, but actual experience is far better.

The foregoing items include those which come under the head of carpentry. Of course the contractor will have many other items on which to figure if he desires to estimate or contract for the entire job.

The following list, arranged in regular order, will

be found to include the principal divisions of estimating an entire job, and also shows a good form for an estimate :

FORM FOR AN ESTIMATE.

	$	¢
Excavating........		
Foundation walls		
Brick walls and piers...........		
Chimneys...........................		
Lumber...................		
Carpentry work..........		
Hardware.............		
Tin work..........		
Galvanized iron work.......		
Plastering................................		
Plumbing......................		
Gas fitting		
Steam fitting.............................		
Painting..................................		
Incidental expenses...........		

PRINCIPAL DIVISIONS IN ESTIMATING.

Under each division there will always appear many items on which to figure, but as contractors are supposed to be supplied with specifications, it is useless to enumerate all the items as they may appear under each head. The two principal divisions of lumber and carpentry have been given in full in every detail of the work. Under the other divisions it will only be necessary to mention a few of the essential points to enable any one to estimate them easily and accurately.

EXCAVATIONS.

Excavating for foundation walls, cellars, cisterns, &c., is estimated by the cubic yard, which contains 27 cubic feet. The rate per yard is variable in different localities and according to the location of the grounds and the hardness of the earth to be excavated.

FOUNDATIONS AND CHIMNEYS.

Foundations are generally laid of brick or stone. Brick are laid by the thousand, and stone by the perch. The rates and customs of measuring are variable in different localities. The following, however, is the usual custom of measuring brick and stone work. For a foundation the outside measurement of the wall is the one taken. To find the number of perches of stone in walls, multiply the length in feet by the hight in feet, and that by the thickness in feet, and divide the product by 22. No allowance is made for openings, unless they are numerous or of considerable size.

EXAMPLE AND SOLUTION.

Take the following example : How many perches of stone in a wall 48 feet long, 8 feet high and 1 foot 6 inches thick? The solution to this is : $48 \times 8 \times 1\frac{1}{2} \div 22 = 26.18$ perches. A perch of stone measures usually 24.75 cubic feet, but when built in a wall 2.75 cubic feet are allowed for mortar and filling. To find the perches of masonry divide the cubic feet by 24.75 instead of 22. In estimating the masonry no allowance is made for openings. A thousand brick are about equal to two perches of stone when laid in a wall. Brick are counted as follows :

For a 4-inch wall 7½ bricks to the foot.
For an 8-inch wall 15 bricks to the foot.
For a 12-inch wall 22½ bricks to the foot.
For a 16-inch wall 30 bricks to the foot.
In estimating for the number of brick the open-

ings may be deducted if they are large or numerous. In the measurement of masonry, however, no deduction is made for openings. Seven hundred and fifty brick laid in a wall are equal to 1000 brick, wall count. The customary price allowed for the labor of laying brick is $2 per 1000, wall count.

A chimney of 1½ by 2 brick makes a flue 4 x 8 inches inside and requires 25 bricks per foot. A chimney of 2 by 2 brick makes a flue 8 x 8 inches inside and requires 30 bricks per foot, while a chimney of 2 by 2½ brick makes a flue 8 x 12 inside and requires 35 bricks per foot. Chimneys of any size may be estimated by counting the number of brick required for one course and allowing five courses to the foot. A chimney breast for a fire place is usually of 2 x 7 brick and requires 80 to 90 bricks per foot.

LATHING AND PLASTERING.

Lathing is estimated by the square yard and the usual rate is 3 cents per yard. Fifteen lath are counted to the yard, and 6½ pounds of threepenny nails per 1000 lath. Plastering is also estimated by the square yard. The lathing and plastering are usually estimated together at the following rates, including material and labor:

For two-coat work, 18 to 23 cents per yard, and for three-coat work, 23 to 27 cents. In the measurement of plastering no deduction is made for openings.

PAINTING.

When a carpenter has to figure upon painting it is better for him to get some reliable mechanic who is in the business to give figures on the work. Painters

figure their work by the square yard. I have in-
quired of practical painters concerning their methods
of calculation and have failed to find any uniform
scale or rule by which to measure surfaces. Nearly
all master painters have a basis of calculation, but the
accuracy of their estimates depends so much upon
personal judgment as to the nature and extent of
variations, that their methods would be useless to
persons of less accurate judgment. The methods
also vary according to the nature of the work and
the training of the painter. No two would measure
in the same way, perhaps, yet they might reach
nearly the same results. Although it is true that
very much depends upon the painter's judgment, I
will try to give a few hints which will be found in
some cases entirely trustworthy and in all helpful.
One way of measuring is to obtain the number of
square feet in the sides and ends of a building as if
they are flat surfaces, give a rough guess as to the
dimensions of trimming, &c., and let it go at that.
This plan may work well for a good guesser, but for
general use it is not very satisfactory. Another way
in connection with wooden buildings is to measure
the length and exposed surface of one strip of siding,
then count the siding and multiply the dimensions
of one by the whole number on the side or end of
the building ; the product will be the surface measure. This is a better way, but its accuracy depends
upon a pretty thorough acquaintance with compound
numbers, as dimensions must be reduced to inches,
then back to feet or yards, according to the basis of
calculation. Trimmings, &c., are measured separately.
   Common siding are put on with one board over-

lapping another, and the lapping edge of the board is raised from the perpendicular, so that it presents a diagonal instead of a flat surface ; and there is also the exposed edge of the board, about ½ inch, which should be included in the estimate. Suppose, now, that the exposed portion of a board of siding is 4 inches—the usual width—and the edge ½ inch. It will give the side of a building just 12½ per cent. more surface than it would possess if it were perfectly flat. Hence one-eighth added to the dimensions, obtained by multiplying hight and length together, will give the actual surface measure of common siding.

In drop siding, which is frequently used, there is an exposed edge of about ½ inch, and about ¼ inch more surface on the molded edge than there would be if it were flat, thus making a total gain over flat surface of ¾ inch on each piece of siding, or 18¾ per cent., which is very nearly equal to one-fifth. Hence one-fifth should be added to the dimensions in square feet of a building to obtain the surface measurement for drop siding.

In measuring the gable ends of ordinary buildings the dimensions should be one-half less than actual square measure. For example, if a building is 20 feet wide, and is 10 feet from the level of the frame plates to the point of the roof, multiply half the width, 10 feet, by the hight, 10 feet, and we have 100 feet surface of the gable end, to which should be added the percentages for the edges of the siding boards, &c. No deduction is usually made for openings. Cornice and trimmings should be measured separately. If there are panels, beads and other projecting and receding features, brackets, &c., carefully measure one of each, count the number on the building and multiply by that number; the product will be the total surface. Open brackets on cornices and scroll and lattice work on verandas should be measured solid, as the edges fully make up for open spaces.

The utter lack of uniformity in house trimmings compels more or less reliance upon the judgment of the painter in measuring them. I can suggest no rule for measuring which can be used with satisfactory results in all cases. What would be admirably suited to one would be wholly unadapted to another, simply because the architectural features are unlike. Here there is no alternative but to exercise judgment in considering these important features.

In calculating the quantity of paint required upon the basis of surface measurement, from 12 to 40 per cent. should be allowed for trimmings, &c., according to their size and shape. For plain work 12 to 20 per cent. will be found a fair average. This depends, however, upon the number of doors and windows, style of frames, &c. On Queen Anne structures, which are painted with two or three body colors and are burdened with numerous and elaborate trimmings, calculations must be made of the portions of the buildings to which the different body colors are to be applied either by divisions of total measurement or by separate measurements and the trimmings considered separately. As outside painting on buildings usually consists of two coats over a previously painted surface, or if on a surface never before painted, preceded by a primary coat, it is customary to estimate the quantity of paint required for two coats. Surfaces are so variable in condition that no rule can be given which will be found applicable to all cases. The quantity of paint required for two-coat work varies from 3½ to 5 gallons per 100 square yards, and I would by all means advise carpenters to obtain figures from experienced painters in this particular line of business.

HARDWARE.

Estimating hardware is as much of a necessity with the carpenter as estimating lumber, but it is not attended with as many variations and difficulties. The number of fixtures for door and window trimmings, &c., may be readily counted from the plans, and it is only through the omission of some items that any serious mistake is likely to happen. A careful study of the plans and a well prepared list of hardware items from which to figure is a guard against mistakes from omissions and a guide to correct estimating.

LIST OF ITEMS FOR ESTIMATING HARDWARE.

Nails, various sizes (see table).

Brads.	Hooks and eyes.
Blind hinges.	Drawer pulls.
Window bolts.	Mortise bolts.
Axle pulleys.	Flush bolts.
Sash locks.	Registers.
Sash cord.	Door stops.
Window weights.	Tin window caps.
Mortise locks.	Tin shingles.
Rim locks.	Valley tin.
Butts, various sizes.	Hip shingles
Parlor door hangers.	Tin roofing.
Wrought butts.	Conductors.
Strap hinges.	Screws.
Transom lifters.	Sandpaper.
Cupboard catches.	Wardrobe hooks

On small jobs old contractors who have learned to judge from experience usually arrive at the quantities of nails by guessing. The following table, however, may be found available to many in estimating nails for various purposes. As wire nails are coming into general use, and are already extensively employed, the basis of estimating has been made on the number of wire nails to the pound. If cut nails are used add one-third to the amount :

TABLE FOR ESTIMATING NAILS.

1000 shingles require $3\frac{1}{2}$ pounds 4d nails.
1000 lath require $6\frac{1}{2}$ pounds 3d nails.
1000 feet of beveled siding requires 18 pounds 6d nails.
1000 feet of sheeting requires 20 pounds 8d nails.
1000 feet of sheeting requires 25 pounds 10d nails.
1000 feet of flooring requires 30 pounds 8d nails.
1000 feet of flooring requires 35 pounds 10d nails.
1000 feet of studding requires 14 pounds 10d nails.
1000 feet of studding requires 10 pounds 20d nails.
1000 feet of furring 1 x 2 requires 10 pounds 10d nails.
1000 feet of $\frac{7}{8}$ finish requires 30 pounds of 8d nails.
1000 feet of $1\frac{1}{8}$ finish requires 40 pounds 10d finish nails.

The following table shows the name, length and number of nails to the pound of the different sizes :

NUMBER OF NAILS TO THE POUND.

Name.	Length.	No. to a pound.
3d fine	1 inch	1150
3d common	$1\frac{1}{4}$ inch	720
4d common	$1\frac{3}{8}$ inch	432
5d common	$1\frac{1}{2}$ to $1\frac{3}{4}$ inch	352
6d finish	2 inch	350
6d common	2 inch	252
7d common	$2\frac{1}{4}$ inch	192
8d finish	$2\frac{1}{2}$ inch	190

Name.	Length.	No. to a pound.
8d common.............	2½ inch......	132
9d common...	2¾ inch....	110
10d finish.........	3 inch....................	137
10d common.. 3	inch....	87
12d common....... ....3¼	inch.......	66
20d common...............3⅝	inch.......	35
80d common..... 4	inch....................	27
40d common...............4½	inch............	21
50d common...............5⅛	inch....................	15
60d common..... 6	inch....................	12
70d common.... 7	inch....................	9

FORM OF CONTRACT.

Articles of Agreement, made on this.............
....day of
.............., A. D. 18........, by and between
...., party of the first part
and........................... ...... , party of the
second part : *Wi nesseth,* That for and in consideration of the money hereinafter stipulated to be paid
to the party of the first part by the party of the
second part, the party of the first part has, and by
these conditions does hereby agree to furnish all
labor and material of every kind and to build and
complete on or by the..................................
.............on the premises of the party of the
second part, situated in........................
a residence as shown upon the drawings and set
forth in the specifications. Said drawings and specifications being verified by the signatures of the parties
are taken as a part of this contract. And the party
of the first part agrees that all material furnished,
or workmanship employed, shall be of the best char-

acter and quality, as mentioned in the said specifications. The party of the first part further agrees that
he will complete, in accordance with the plans and
specifications, to the full and entire satisfaction of
the party of the second part, all the work that is to
be done by the ....

In consideration of which the party of the second
part agrees to pay to the party of the first part the
sum of $.......... as follows :

When the foundations are completed.... $........
When the entire building is under roof.. $........
When the entire building is plastered.... $........
When the entire building is completed... $........

*In Witness Whereof, the parties hereto have affixed
their signatures :*

....[L. S.]

............................[L. S]

Witness :...............................

PRACTICAL METHODS OF CONSTRUCTION.

As most carpenters are familiar with the usual methods of construction in the line of carpentry, I will only mention a few points on this subject, which seem to me to be more or less neglected.

MAKING CORNERS.

It is customary, nowadays, to make the outside corners of many buildings by simply doubling and spiking two studding together, as shown by section in Fig. 48. By this method there is nothing to receive the lath from one side, and as soon as the lathers begin work, the carpenter is called upon either to put in another studding or the lather puts in anything he can find to which to nail the lath. In many instances it is nothing more than a double thickness of lath nailed up and down the corner. This does not make a solid corner, and as a consequence the plastering soon cracks, even before the carpenter is through finishing. It is almost impossible to put down the base in a house constructed with such corners without cracking them, simply because they are not solid. Fig. 49 shows a section of a corner which is a much better method of construction, and one which makes a solid corner. The

Fig. 48.—An Outside Corner.

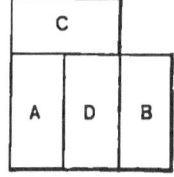

Fig. 49.—Section of a Corne·, Indicating a Better Method of Construction than sh·wn in Previous Figure.

64

corner is made of three studding, A, B, C, spiked together as shown. D is an open space between A and B, which may be filled in with blocks. Corners constructed in this way make solid nailing for the lath and base from both sides. Figs. 50 and 51 show two forms for making solid corners for partition angles by using three studding.

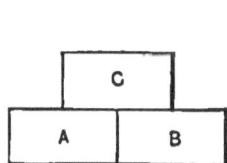

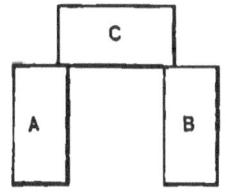

Fig 50. Method of Making Solid Corners for Partition Angle.

Fig. 51.—Another Method of Making Solid Corners.

If it is desired to save studding a board can be nailed to the back of studding C, which will often answer the purpose. It is a very common thing for carpenters in setting partitions to place the studding joining another partition half an inch away from it, so that the lather may run the lath through back of the partition studding, as shown in Fig. 52. This does not make a solid corner and is a very poor method of construction.

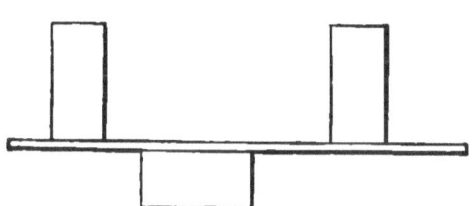

Fig 52.—Showing Improper Manner of Running the Lath.

SPACING STUDDING.

As the second floor joists in buildings usually rest on a ribbon board framed into the studding, it is

necessary that the studding on both sides of the building on which the joists have their bearing should be
regularly spaced.   Many are in the habit of laying
off the openings and spacing the studding to conform
thereto.   This method causes great irregularity of
spacing, making some wide and some narrow spaces,
which either bring the joists overhead out of position

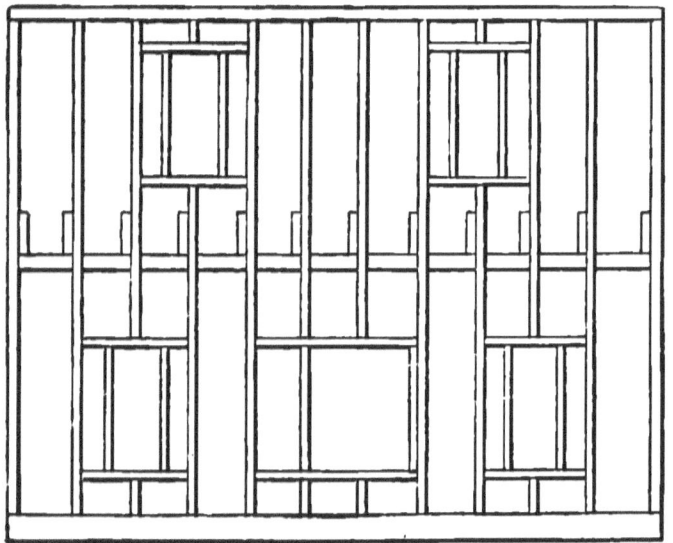

Fig. 53.—Showing Proper Method of Spacing Studding.

or leaves them standing alone on the ribbon without
any means of being properly fastened.

Studding should be spaced regardless of the openings, after which the openings may be laid out and
the necessary studding may be cut and headers put
in, as shown in Fig. 53. This method leaves the
studding all regularly spaced, and the joists will all
nail to the side of a studding and come in the proper
order.   Now, if the studding are set to conform to

the openings, as shown in Fig. 54, it breaks up the regular order of spacing, leaving some spaces wide and some narrow. It will also be noticed that we have two more studding spaced on the sill and plate than in Fig. 53. It is, therefore, evident that if the joists are regularly spaced many of them will stand alone on the ribbon board, with no place to properly

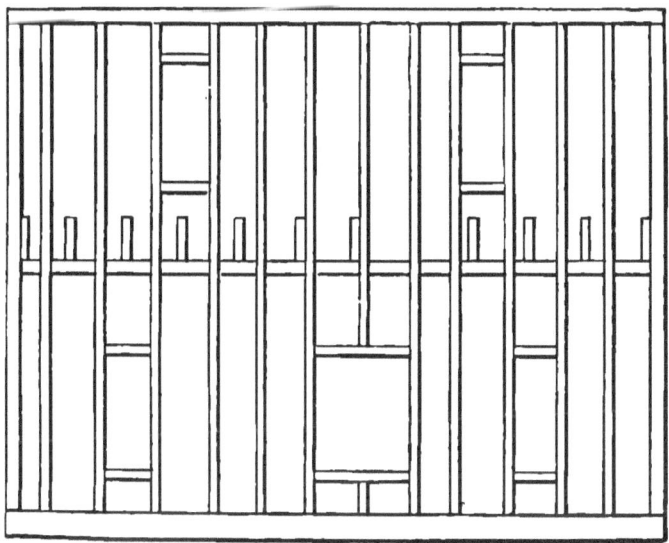

Fig. 54.—Showing Studding Set to Conform to Openings.

fasten them, as shown. If they are placed over to the side of the studding, as they frequently are, then they are thrown off their centers and the spacing is wrong.

CORNER BLOCKS.

Every workman has experienced more or less diffi-culty in nailing up corner blocks in casing doors and windows. The trouble all comes from the want of a solid background on which to nail the blocks. Very often the plastering is not finished level and true with the jambs. All trouble with corner blocks may be avoided by taking a common board of the proper thickness, 1½ inches narrower than the inside head casing, 1½ inches shorter than the width of window and side casings, and nail it tight down on the head jamb, as shown in Fig. 55. By this method the corner blocks will nail up true and solid without cracking the plastering. Care should be taken that the board is not too wide nor too long, as the blocks and head casing should completely cover it from view.

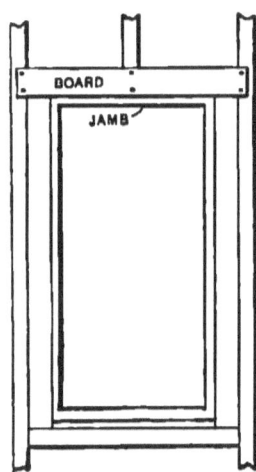

Fig. 55 —Method of Putting up Corner Blocks.

MITERING AND COPING BASE.

Many mechanics have probably experienced more or less difficulty in mitering and coping base, particularly of the hardwood finish and molded-edge patterns. There are two distinct kinds of joints to make in putting down base. The angles which form the four sides of a room are called internal angles, and the joints should always be coped. The projecting corners of a chimney, or any corners projecting into a room, are termed external angles, and the joints should always be mitered. To cope a joint in putting down base, cut and fit in square the first piece. Cut the piece which is to be coped to the other about 1½ inches longer than the actual length needed; place it as nearly as possible in position, and with the dividers set to about the thickness of the base, scribe down by the side of the piece already fitted and nailed in place; then scribe all the parts which are easy. Beads and molded surfaces which are difficult to scribe, prick with the dividers near the center of each member ; cut the square part of base as usual, but cut the molded part on an angle which will just touch all the points made by the dividers. This will give the true line for coping. After cutting the base to the coping line, first see that the joint will fit, as sometimes a little trimming is necessary; then obtain the proper length, cut off and place the board in position, putting in last when possible to do so the end which is coped. By this method a joint can be made very tight without the annoyance of the other end of the board scraping into the plastering. Many carpenters use a templet for obtaining the cut which gives the coping line. It, however, is of little use, as it is always made with the supposition that all angles are square and true, which is far from being the case. Scribing and cutting as above described is far better, as it will make a joint to fit any angle, and with a little practice a perfect fit will be obtained at the first cut.

To miter base around external angles, mark the proper miter on the square edge of the base and square across on the back side and the square part of the face side. Cut from the top edge of base, starting on back line and cutting on an angle which will just cut the line on the square part of the face side. A little practice will convince any one that a templet for cutting base is not really worth carrying around. When properly basing a chimney, fit all the joints before nailing, and then clamp all the pieces in their proper places by nailing blocks on the floor and driving in braces. One will be surprised at what a neat job can be done and how easy it is to do it. There will not be the usual difficulty in driving the nails, and cracked and mutilated chimney corners will not bear evidence of a bad job of basing around them. The great difficulty of driving nails into the bricks is largely overcome by having the work clamped tightly against it.

BINDING SLIDING DOORS.

I have frequently noticed that a remedy is wanted for binding sliding doors. This question is very frequently asked, and it is not to be wondered at, for not one sliding door in ten put up works in anything like a satisfactory manner. I have had a great deal of experience with sliding doors, and am pretty well acquainted with the common defects and causes of unsatisfactory working. I do not wonder that a good remedy is wanted for these troublesome doors, for unless they work properly they become a great inconvenience. The causes of the unsatisfactory working of sliding doors are many, and a little general information on the subject may not come amiss. Nearly all the causes of the imperfect working of sliding doors can be traced directly to the improper construction of some part of the work in putting them up, and in most cases an ounce of prevention is worth about 4 pounds of the cure. As overhead hangers are almost exclusively used these are the ones we will take into consideration. First, it is necessary that the floor under sliding-door partitions should be perfectly solid and very nearly level.

It is a common occurrence for buildings to settle, and if partitions, which often have a great weight to support, are not provided with a properly constructed foundation, they will settle enough to throw the ordinary sliding door entirely out of working order. It will not do to block up under sliding-door partitions with a little chip, a piece of a shingle, a little loose dirt under a post in the cellar bottom or some fresh mortar, as is often practiced. As the increased weight of the plastering and floors is put upon the partitions above, the floors begin to settle. I have seen floors under sliding doors ¾ inch out of level. How can sliding doors work when put up under such circumstances? If the track was level, one door would be sure to strike the floor as it was rolled back, while the other door would rise almost 1½ inches from the floor. Again, if the track was not level, but placed parallel with the floor, then the doors could not be adjusted to hang plumb; consequently, they would not fit the jambs, unless the jambs were set to fit the doors ¾ inch out of plumb.

Thus far we see that the floor must be perfectly solid and level, the partitions must be set plumb, the headers put in solid and of sufficient strength to carry all the weight placed upon them without yielding or sagging. We will now turn our attention to the putting up of the track. This should be level and straight, and it should be straight sideways as well as on top where the rollers run. This is a point overlooked by many. They think if the track is straight on top that is all that is necessary, but short kinks sideways in a track will cause the doors to run crooked—running away from the stops on one side of the jamb, and crowding them on the other, often causing binding. Again, most hangers require a double track, constructed in the following manner: The track is 1 x 1¼ inches, and screwed to the edge of a board ⅞ x 6 inches. These boards are then fastened to the partitions at the proper hight for the doors, and another piece 4¾ inches wide, called a spreader, is placed over the top. The sketch, Fig. 56, gives a

general idea of the construction of the track and boxing. In the diagram it will be noticed that the opening between the tracks and between the jambs,
through which the lower part of the door hanger
passes, is only one inch wide. The hangers have small

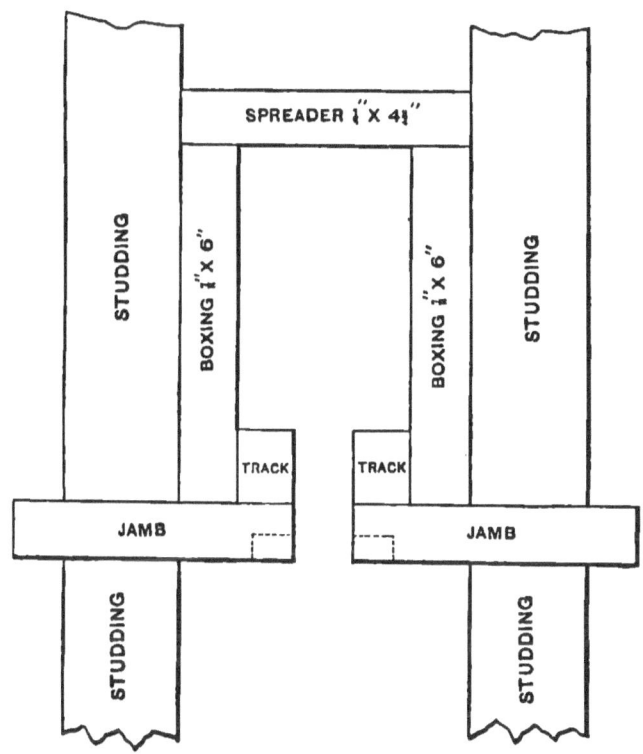

Fig. 56.—Section showing Construction of Track and Boxing for
Sliding Doors.

friction rollers, which run between the two tracks,
serving as a guide for the wheels above, and not leaving more than ⅛ inch play between the two tracks.
This ⅛ inch is plenty of room if the work is properly
done. It is necessary that the friction rollers run

close to the track in order that the doors may run true and without crowding the door stops. But suppose the boxing is insecurely fastened to the studding, and the dampness from the plastering, when it is put on, causes the two 6-inch boards to cup. The tendency at once is to narrow the opening required by the friction rollers of the hangers, thus causing a binding of the door hangers between the two tracks. Again, suppose the spreader, which is for the sole purpose of keeping the tracks the right distance apart, is carelessly put in a little narrow, or, perhaps, left out entirely, as it is occasionally by some, who consider it an unnecessary appendage to the working of sliding doors, then there is practically nothing to keep the tracks from springing together, causing a binding of the doors.

Again, if the spreader is narrow or left out, the continual pounding of the lathers on the partition walls, and the carpenters in finishing, have a tendency to drive the partitions a little closer together, especially if they are not securely fastened at the top. Fully as many binding sliding doors are caused by the tracks springing together as in any other way, and when from this cause, the remedy is a difficult one to apply, as the doors may have to be taken down and the sides of the track trimmed off with very long-handled, sharp-edged tools. This cause of binding is likely to be overlooked, as it is the least suspected, and comes very near being an invisible cause. Again, we will suppose that a building being erected is to have sliding doors—that the tracks are put in level and at the proper time. Now, after the building has been plastered and the carpenter comes

to finish the sliding doors, he finds that the weight
of the plastering or something has caused the floor
to settle and the track is out of level. Well, about
nine carpenters out of ten will put the head-jamb
level, which will bring one end of the jamb down
from the track just as much as the floor is out of
level. The consequence is that when the doors slide
back, one of them will rub the head-jamb and quite
likely stick fast. The head-jamb belongs snug up to
the bottom edge of the track, as shown in Fig. 56,
and there is where it should be placed, even if the
track is out of level. To level the head-jamb when
the track is not level only makes matters worse. A
doorway with the head-jamb slightly out of level
will not be noticed, but a door that will stick fast
will be noticed every time it is opened. Of course I
advocate doing the work correctly in the first place,
and am now showing what to do in cases of emer-
gency. Sometimes it is necessary to rabbet the head-
jambs at the lower portion of the inside edge, as
shown by the dotted lines in Fig. 56. Again, some
workmen do not plow the groove in the bottom edge
of the door deep enough for the floor guide. It
might work when the door was first fitted, but a
little settling of the track would cause binding of the
door. This can be easily remedied by letting the
floor guide into the floor, or by taking the door down
and plowing the groove deeper. The former is the
easiest and quickest and in every way just as good.
The binding of sliding doors is often caused by the
door stops being placed too close to the doors.
When this is the case a removal of the stops and

placing them a little farther away will remedy the trouble.

In hanging sliding doors it is better, if possible, to do so before the jambs are set. Many times little things that would interfere with the proper working of the doors can be easily remedied ; whereas, if the jambs were set, they would be concealed from general view and not discovered until they had caused a considerable amount of trouble. Is there any difference in door hangers? is a question which very naturally arises. In our estimation there is considerable difference, although any of them, I think, would give satisfaction if every part of the work in putting them up was done in a substantial manner. Some hangers have more points of excellence than others, but I think the Prescott hanger the nearest perfection. With this hanger there is no track and no rollers. The doors hang suspended from the back edge, the hangers being fastened to the studding back of the jambs. They are as nearly frictionless as a door swinging on hinges, and there is no binding of doors from tracks and rollers. In fact, there is no more chance for the doors to bind from settling partitions than there is with the ordinary swinging doors on common hinges. Of the double-track overhead hangers, I think the Annex a very good specimen. All parts of the hanger are accurately fitted and the adjustment is as good as could be desired. The Standard door hanger is another good specimen, and I think sometimes it will allow doors to work free and easy under circumstances which other overhead hangers would not.

TO PREVENT LEAKS IN BAY WINDOWS.

It seems to be a very difficult matter for a carpenter to build a bay window that will not leak in a
bad rain storm. There are comparatively few bays
built that do not have a window or a large double window directly over them, and the leak is almost invari-
ably down the side of the casings of these windows.
The bay window may be well roofed and the tin
turned up under the siding for 5 or 6 inches, yet it
will leak, and where the water gets in will be a mys-
tery to a close observer. Water-tight joints are not
always made in siding, and sometimes the casings
shrink from the siding ; then the rain beats in by the
side of the casing of the upper windows and runs
down behind the tin turned up from the roof, thus
causing a leak. To prevent this, saw through the sheeting under the window casings and to about 6 inches
each side, slanting the same upward in sawing. Now
put a piece of tin well into the saw kerf, and bend it
down over the tin that turns up from the roof ; then,
after the siding is properly put on, we have a bay
window that is positively water tight. Care should
be taken in siding and not drive nails too near the
roof. It is better to slant them a little upward in
driving. In no case should the sills of the upper
windows come closer than 4½ inches to the roof of
the bay window, as it is necessary to have room for
the tin to insure a good job.

SHINGLING HIPS AND VALLEYS.

There are several methods of shingling hips and
valleys, but as most mechanics are familiar with the
different methods, I will briefly describe only a few

of the best and most practical ones.   In shingling
hips both sides should be shingled up at the same
time, and on hip roofs of unequal pitch it is necessary to lay the shingles more to the weather on the
long side of roof than on the short side, in order to
have the courses member evenly on the hip.   One
method frequently employed is to cut the hip shingles
so that the straight edge of the shingles will line with
the center of the hip when laid, and the grain of the
wood run parallel with the hip instead of straight
up the roof, as in the case of common shingles. Some
are inclined to think this method makes a nicer looking job than the o'd way of placing the sawed edge
of hip shingle to the hip line.   As it is customary to
use tin hip shingles, I think the old way is by far the
best, as the water which falls on the roof will run
with the grain of the wood, and not soak into the
shingles, as it would running diagonally across the
grain.

The same is true in shingling valleys.   Always
place the valley shingles with the grain of the wood
running up the roof the same as the common shingles, then the water running down the roof to the
valley will run with the grain of the wood.   Some
trouble is experienced in shingling valleys straight.
The usual custom is to put in a strip of 14-inch tin
for the valley, and strike two chalk lines, leaving a
space in the center of the valley 2 inches wide at the
top and 3 inches at the bottom for the valley.   It is
a very particular job to shingle to a chalk line up a
valley and shingle it straight.   Then again, the line
will be rubbed out before the shingling is half done.
A better way is to stand a 2 x 4 up edgewise in the

valley, fasten it straight with a few pieces of shingles for braces and shingle to the 2 x 4, which answers as a straight edge. In this way one will get a respectable looking valley, even when shingled by inexperienced hands. I have frequently seen valleys which some one had tried to shingle to a line that were at least 2 inches crooked, and between 5 and 6 inches wide in places, generally wider in the middle than at either end. Wide valleys should be avoided, as they are very liable to leak. In shingling a valley no nails should be driven through the valley tin except near the outer edge, as a nail hole will frequently cause a leak by water getting under the shingles. The best way to shingle a valley is to use single sheets of tin 10 x 14 inches, under each of the courses of shingles, leaving only about ¼ inch of the tin exposed below the butts of the shingles. Make a close joint with them in the valley, and a good as well as neat looking job will be the result when the work is finished. To increase the durability of the valley, paint the tin flashings before laying.

ART OF ROOF FRAMING.

Probably no part in the construction of buildings so thoroughly taxes the skill and ingenuity of the builder as the framing of roofs. Many diagrams have been published from time to time showing how to find the lengths and bevels of hips, valleys and jacks on all kinds of roofs. Yet many of the plans heretofore published have been too complicated to satisfy the wants of the inexperienced in the art of roof framing. At this time will be presented a choice of methods, beginning with the simplest form and illustrating the subject step by step, thus showing new and novel plans as they will appear in actual practice.

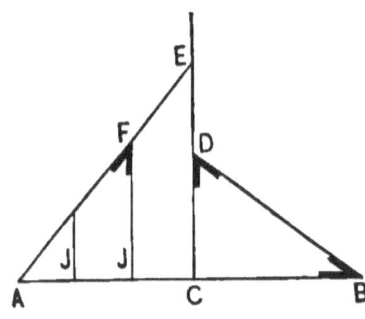

Fig. 57.—Obtaining Lengths and Bevels of Rafters.

First will be introduced a plan showing how to obtain the lengths and bevels of common rafters, hips, valleys and jacks in the simplest manner, and with the fewest lines possible. Referring to Fig. 57, draw a horizontal line twice the run of the common rafter, as A B. From the center of this line at C erect a perpendicular, continuing it indefinitely. Next set off on the perpendicular the rise of the common rafter C D; connect D and B for the length of the common rafter. A bevel set in the angle at B will give the bottom cut and at D the top cut. Next

80

set off on the perpendicular line the length of the
common rafter C E, which is the same length as D
B. Connect E and A for the length of the hip or
valley, as the case may be. Next space the jacks on
the line A C and draw perpendicular lines joining
the hip or valley. The lines J J will be the lengths
of the jacks, and a bevel set in the angle at F, where
the jack joins the hip or valley, will give the bevel
across the back of the same. The plumb cut or
down bevel of a jack is always the same as that of
the common rafter. There are now shown all the
lines necessary to be drawn, the plan indicating
everything but the cuts
of the hip or valley
rafter, and this, be it remembered, is always 17
for the bottom cut and
the rise of the common
rafter to the foot run for
the top cut. As some may
think a system which
does not show the cuts
of a hip or valley as well

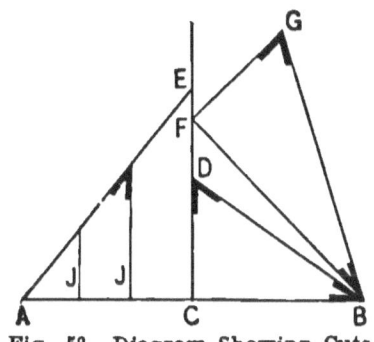

Fig. 58.—Diagram Showing Cuts
of Hip or Valley Rafters.

as its length is incomplete, we will take the same
plan and by the addition of three more lines show
everything that can be desired, as in Fig. 58. Draw
the lines the same as in Fig. 57, then set off on the
perpendicular line the run of the common rafter
C F. Connect F and B for run of hip or valley.
Next square up the rise from F to G and connect G
and B for the length of hip or valley rafter. A bevel
set in the angle at B will give the bottom cut, and at
G the top cut. It will be noticed in Fig. 58 that the

lines A E and G B are of the same length, and in both
cases represent the hip or valley, while showing it in
different positions. The line A E shows the hip or
valley in position for finding the length and bevel of
the jacks, while the line G B shows the hip or valley
in position to find the length and bevels of the
same. This plan will work on roofs of any pitch and
has only to be slightly varied to meet the require
ments of roofs having
hips and valleys of two
pitches. On half pitch
roofs one less line is required, as shown in Fig.
59. The line D B in Fig.
58 comes in the same po-
sition as F B, when ap-
plied to half pitch roofs,
and is t h e r e f o r e the
length of the common
rafter and at the same
time represents the run
of the hip rafter. As two lines cannot be drawn in
the same space we drop the line D B, remembering
that it is shown by F B.

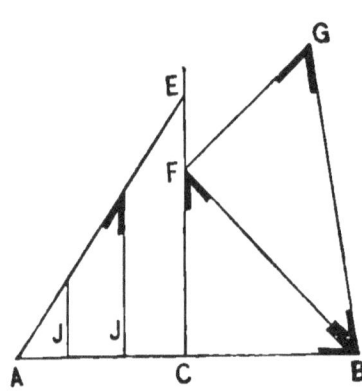

Fig. 59.—Diagram for Half Pitch
Roofs.

BEVEL OF JACK RAFTERS.

Before proceeding further with the subject of roof
framing we will illustrate a very simple method for
obtaining the bevel across the back of jack rafters,
or any rafter which cuts on a bevel across the back.
Referring to Fig. 6o, draw the plumb line or pitch of
the roof on the side of the rafter B C. Next draw
another plumb line the thickness of the rafter from
the first, and measured square from B C, as shown

by the dotted lines. Square across the back of the rafter, from the dotted plumb line to A. Connect A with B, and the lines to follow in cutting are A B C. This plan is worth remembering, as it will work on roofs of any pitch, and, in fact, will cut the bevel across the back of any rafter which cuts on a bevel. It is the plumb cut and the thickness of the rafter applied in the manner described that does the business every time. After the cuts have been found bevels can be set for them if desired.

BACKING HIP RAFTERS.

Let us now consider the backing of the hip rafter, an item which on common house and barn framing is of but little importance, yet it is well enough to know how it

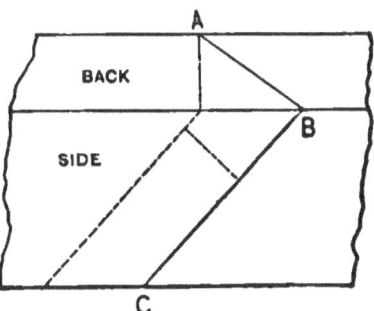

Fig. 60.—Obtaining Bevel Across the Back of Jack Rafters.

is done. Almost any roof is as good without as with the hips backed, and when the roof is completed it is impossible to tell which method was pursued. In cases where the hip rafter is doubled or very thick it is advisable to back it, but ordinarily this is unnecessary, being a waste of time. Where backing is necessary, a rule near enough for all practical purposes is as follows : Working from the center of the back of rafter set the bevel to cut off

$\frac{5}{8}$ inch in 1 inch for three-fourth pitch roofs.

$\frac{1}{2}$ inch in 1 inch for one-half pitch roofs.

$\frac{3}{8}$ inch in 1 inch for one-third pitch roofs.

$\frac{1}{4}$ inch in 1 inch for one-quarter pitch roofs.

As the above table may not be considered a scientific way of doing the work, Fig. 61 is presented. Draw a horizontal line, A B, and from A draw another at an angle representing the bottom cut of the hip rafter, as A C. On the line A C square up the thickness of the rafter to D. Mark the center and draw the line C F at an angle of 45° to A D. On the line E F square up from E to G, and the lines

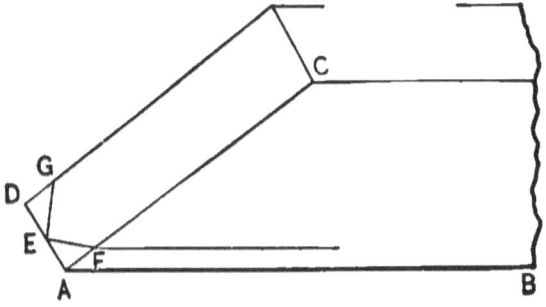

Fig. 61.—Backing a Hip Rafter.

for the backing are G E F. The other lines are merely to show that the piece is off the bottom end of the hip rafter itself.

HIP ROOFS OF UNEQUAL PITCHES.

In Fig. 62 is shown the manner in which the method represented in Fig. 58 may be varied to meet the requirements of roofs of unequal pitches. Draw the line A B, in length equal to the runs of the common rafters on both the long and short sides of the hips. Divide the line A B so that A C will represent the run of the common rafter on the long side of the hip, and C B the run of the common rafter on the short side. From C erect a perpendicular line, extending it indefinitely. Set off on the perpendicular line the rise of the common rafter C D. Connect D with A and with B for the lengths of the common rafters. A bevel set at D on line A D will give the top cut of common rafter on the long side of hip and at A the bottom cut. A bevel set at D on line B D will give the top cut of common rafter on the short side of hip and at B the bottom cut. Next set off on the perpendicular line the length of the common rafter on the short side of the hip C E. Connect E with A for the length of the hip and position for finding the length and bevel of jacks on the short side of the hip.

A bevel set in the angle where they join the hip line A E will give the bevel across the back. The plumb cut or down bevel is the same as that of the common rafter on the short side of the

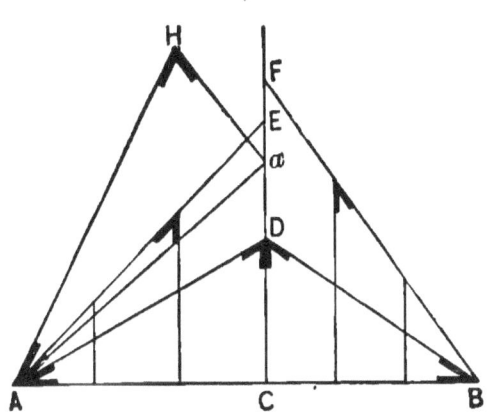

Fig. 62.—Diagram Showing how Method Presented in Fig. 58 may be Varied for Roofs of Unequal Pitches.

hip shown at D on the line D B. Next set off on perpendicular the length of common rafter on the long side of hip C F; connect F with B for the hip and position for finding the length and bevel of jacks on the long side of the hip. A bevel set in the angle where they join the hip line F B will give the bevel across the back. The plumb cut or down bevel is the same as that of the common rafter on the long side of the hip, shown at D on the line A D. To find the cut of the hip rafter set off

on the perpendicular the run of the common rafter
on the short side of hip C *a*. Connect *a* with A for
the run of the hip. Square up the rise of the hip *a* H
and connect H with A for the hip rafter. A bevel
set in the angle at H will give the top cut and at A
the bottom cut. It will be noticed that the lines, B F,
A E and A H show the length of the hip rafters.
B F shows hip rafter in position for finding the length
and bevel of the jacks on the long side of the hip.
A E shows the hip in position for finding the length
and bevel of the jacks on the short side of the hip.
A H shows the hip in position for finding the length
and bevel of the hip rafter. For plain hips and valleys on roofs of equal pitch no one could wish for an
easier method than represented in Fig. 58, but Fig.
62, which has been modified to meet the requirements
of roofs of unequal pitches, necessarily makes the
method more complicated, and with beginners there is
much danger of making mistakes by taking measurements and bevels on the wrong side, as the lengths
of jacks for the long side of roof appear on the short
run of common rafter, and *vice versa* the jacks for the
short side of roof. This circumstance may seem
somewhat strange, yet it is nevertheless true, and
can perhaps be more fully demonstrated by Fig. 63.

GREAT CIRCLE OF JACK RAFTERS.

The great circle of jack rafters is another modifica-
tion of Fig. 58 for roofs of unequal pitches. Referring to Fig. 63, let A B represent the long run of
common rafter, B E the rise and A E the length.
A bevel set at E on the line A E will give the down
bevel and at A the bottom bevel. B C is the short

run of common rafters, B E the rise and C E the length. A bevel set at E on the line C E will give the down bevel and at C the bottom bevel. B D is the short run of the common rafter and the same as B C ; then A D is the angle and run of the hip,

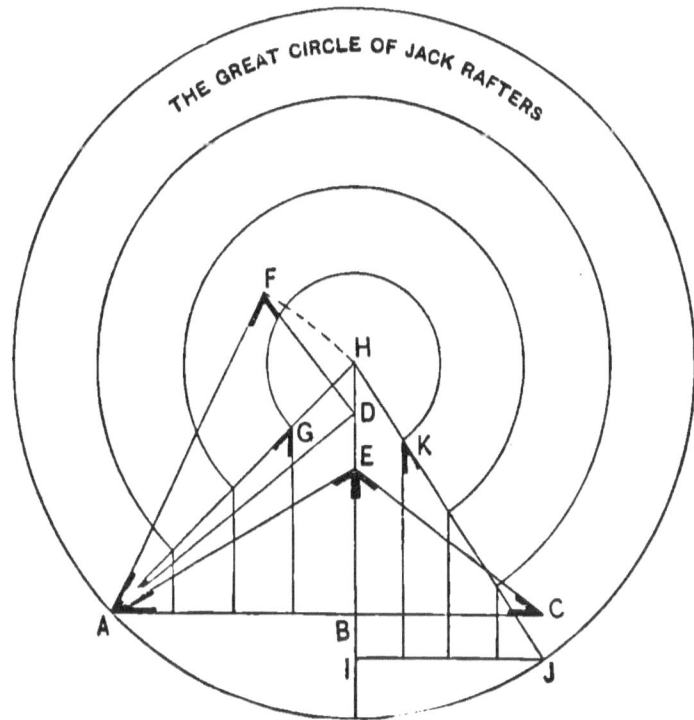

Fig. 63.—Great Circle of Jack Rafters.

D F the rise, and A F the length of hip rafter. The bevel at F is the down bevel and at A the bottom bevel. A H shows the hip rafter A F dropped down in position to find the length and bevel of the jacks for the side of roof having the short run of common rafter. Space the jacks on the line A B and draw perpendicular lines joining the hip line A H for the length of jacks. A bevel set in the angle at G will give the bevel across the back. The down bevel is the same as that of the common rafter for the short run and is shown at E on the line C E. H is the apex of the triangle formed on the side of the roof having the short run of common rafter. It is evident that the apex of the triangle formed on the side of the roof having the long run of the common rafter must be at the same point, therefore H is the apex of the hip and of the common rafters from either side of the hip. Now, to find the length and bevel of jacks on the side of roof having the long run of common rafter, measure down from H to I the length of the common rafter on the long run, which is the same as A E. From I set off the short run of common rafter to J ; connect J with H, which places the hip rafter in position for finding the length and bevel of jacks on the side of roof having the long run of common rafter. Space the jacks on the line I J and draw perpendicular lines, joining the hip line J H, which gives the length of jacks. A bevel set in the angle at K will give the bevel across the back. The down bevel is the same as that of the common rafter for the long run, and is shown at E on the line A E. The circular lines show that taking H as a center the triangle H I J will swing around opposite the triangle A B H, and bring every jack opposite its mate on the hip line A H, thus proving the correctness of the method, as well as showing how to space the jacks correspondingly.

In Fig. 64 is shown another method for obtaining the lengths and cuts of rafters in hip roofs of unequal pitch. Let A B C represent the wall plate and

D E F the deck plate; then A E is the run of the common rafter on the short side of the hip, E D the rise and A D the length.

The bevel at D is the plumb cut at the top and at A the bottom cut. From A set off the length of the common rafter to G, which should be the same length as A D. Connect B G, which places the hip rafter in position to find the length and bevel of jacks on the short side of the hip. Space the jacks on the line B A, and draw perpendicular lines joining the hip line B G for the length of the jacks on the short side of the hip. The bevel at J is the bevel across the back of the same. The plumb cut or down bevel is the same as that of the common rafter shown at D. C E is the run of the common rafter on the long side of the hip, E F being the rise and C F the length. The bevel at F is the plumb cut at the top and at C the bottom cut. From C set off the length of the common rafter to H, which should be the same length as C F. Connect B H, which places the hip rafter in position to find length and bevel of jacks on the long side of the hip. Space the jacks on the line B C and draw the same, joining the hip line B H, which will give the length of jacks on the long side of the hip. The bevel at K is the bevel across the back. The plumb cut or down bevel is the same as that of the common rafter shown at F. B E is the angle and run of the hip, E I the rise and B I the length of the hip rafter. The bevel at I is the plumb cut at the top and at B the bottom cut fitting the plate. Now, the lines B G, B H and B I show the hip rafter in three different positions for finding the length and bevels of the jacks and the hip, and are practically

the same as shown in Fig. 62.   Of the two plans Fig.
64 is perhaps plainer and more easily understood, yet
both have the common difficulty, a confusion of cross
lines, which is very bothersome to many who are try-
ing to master the art of roof framing.   To make this
system of roof framing so plain that even the most
inexperienced may readily master it, we will show

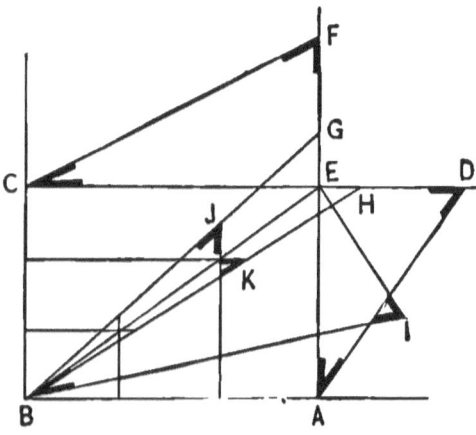

Fig. 61.—Another Method of Obtaining Lengths and Cuts of Rafters
in Hip Roofs of Unequal Pitches.

how the first simple method, Fig. 57, may be further
extended to meet the requirements of any roof, showing all the rafters without the usual complications
of cross lines.   The plan never fails on roofs of any
pitch, equal or unequal, and, no matter how complicated the roof may be, it will all appear easy by this
method.

COMPLICATED ROOF FRAMING MADE EASY.

Let us now take the plan of a hip roof building
having a long run of common rafter on one side of
the hip and a short run on the opposite side.   This

kind of a hip is called an irregular hip, because the base line or run of the hip is not on an angle of 45° with the plates, as in the regular hip. In Fig. 65 A B is the run of common rafter on the left side of the hip and the long run. B D is the run of common rafter on the right side of the hip and the short run, A D being the run of the hip rafter. Now, to make everything plain and avoid the confusion of

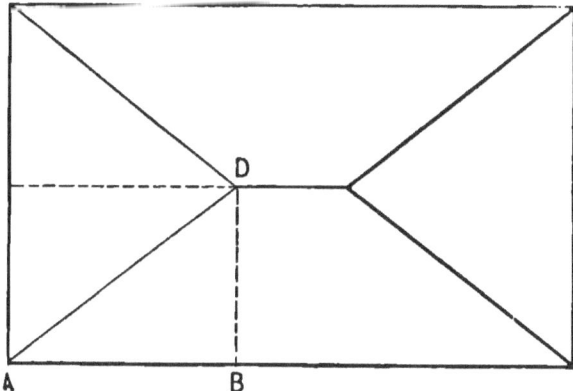

Fig. 65.—Plan of an Irregular Hip Roof.

cross lines which are so troublesome to the inexperienced it is better to make separate diagrams showing each succeeding step as the plan progresses until all is made clear; then one can adopt the plan of separate diagrams or he can combine the whole in one if desired. To beginners separate diagrams are recommended, especially in connection with complicated roofs.

Referring now to Fig. 66, A B is the run of common rafter on the left side of the hip, B E the rise of roof and A E the length of common rafter for the long run. A bevel set in the angle at E will be the plumb cut or down bevel at the top, and a bevel set at A will give the bottom cut fitting the plate. Next set off the run of common rafter on the right side of the hip, B C, and connect E with C for the length of the common rafter for the short run. A bevel set in the angle at E will give the down bevel at the top and at C the bottom cut. We will now proceed to find the hip rafter and bevels for cutting the same. A B is the run of the common rafter on the left side of the hip, B D the run of common rafter on right side of hip, while A D is the run and angle the hip makes with the plates. From D square up the rise of the roof to F; connect F with A, and we have the length of hip rafter. A bevel set in the angle at F will give the down bevel at the top and at A the bottom bevel fitting the plate.

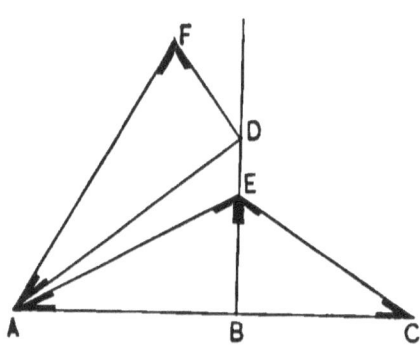

Fig. 66.—Diagram for Finding the Lengths and Bevels of Rafters for Irregular Hip Roofs.

The next step will be to show the length and bevels of the jack rafters. Referring now to Fig. 67, draw a horizontal line, as A C, representing the length of plate in the plan. From A set off the run of the common rafter on the left or long run to B. From B erect a perpendicular to F, which is the length of common rafter on the short run and shown by E C in Fig. 66. Connect F with A, and the hip line is in position for finding the lengths and bevels of the jacks on the side of the building having the short run of common rafter.   Space the jacks on the line A B and draw perpendicular lines joining the hip line.   This will give the lengths of jacks, and a bevel set in the angle at G will give the bevel across the back of the same   The plumb cut or down bevel will be the same as that of the common rafter on the sh rt run.   F D shows the length of ridge and the space which the common rafters oc-

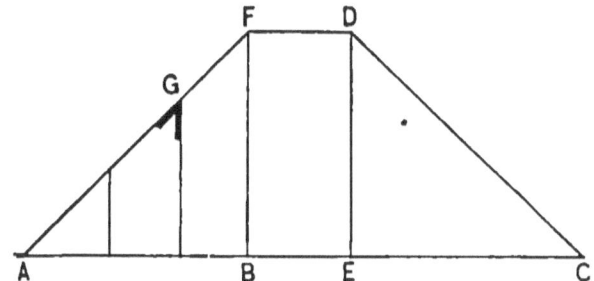

Fig. 67 —Lengths and Levels of Jack Rafters.

cupy.   C E D shows a space for jacks similar to A B F.   It is unnecessary to draw the jacks in this space, and it is therefore left blank.   The next step will be to find the lengths and bevels of the jacks on the end of the building having the long run of the common rafter.   Referring to Fig. 68, let A C represent the width of the building, A B the run of the common rafter on short run, B F the length of common rafter on long run : nd he same as shown by A E in Fig. 66.   Space the line A B for the jacks and draw perpendicular lines joining the hips.   A bevel set in the angle at L will give the bevel across the

back.   The plumb cut or down bevel will be the
same as that of the common rafter on the long run.
Now everything desired has been shown, and with
out the confusion of cross-lines.   By this method all
complications in roof
framing are made easy.
And the most difficult
roofs will show the su-
periority of this plan, as it
is rarely ever necessary
to cross a line, and if
necessary every rafter
may be shown. For roofs
having hips and gables of
varying pitches this plan
has no equal. In Fig. 69
is shown how Figs. 66, 67

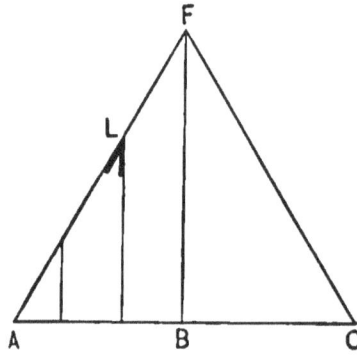

Fig. 68.—Finding Lengths and
Bevels of Jack Rafters on the
End of Building Having the
long run of the Common Rafter.

and 68 may be combined to indicate the differe t
lengths and cuts of all the rafters directly from the
plan.

    This method is attended with many cross lines and
is not recommended even to the most experienced,
for, in connection with complicated roofs, there is
danger of making mistakes. Referring to the plan,
Fig. 69, A B is the run of the common rafter on the
left side of the hip, and the long run B E is the rise,
A E being the length.   A bevel set at E on the line
A E will give the plumb cut or down bevel, and at
A the bottom bevel.   B C is the run of the common
rafter on the right side of the hip, and the short run
B E the rise and E C the length.   A bevel set at E,
on the line C E, will give the plumb cut or down bevel,
and at C the bottom bevel.

A B is the long run of the common rafter, B D the short run of the common rafter, A D the angle and run of the hip, D F the rise of the hip and A F the length of hip rafter. The bevel at F is the down bevel and at A the bottom bevel. B H is the length of the common rafter for the short

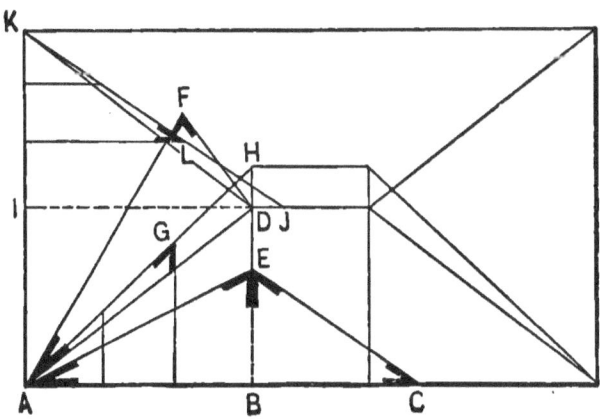

Fig. 69.—Showing how several Diagrams may be combined to indicate directly from the Plan the different Length and Cuts of all the Rafters.

run and the same as C E, while A H is the hip dropped down in position for finding lengths and bevel for jacks on the side of the roof having the short run of the common rafter. The jacks are spaced on the line A B and drawn perpendicular, joining the hip line A H. A bevel set in the angle at G will give the bevel across the back.

The plumb cut or down bevel is the same as that of the common rafter on the short run, and is shown at E on the line E. C. The letters I J represent the length of the common rafter for the long run, which is

the same as A E ; then J K is the length and position
of the hip for finding lengths and bevel for the back
of the jacks on the side having the long run of the
common rafter. Space the jacks on the line I K and
draw them at right angles joining the hip line K J.
A bevel set in the angle at L will give the bevel
across the back of the same, the down bevel being
the same as that of the common rafter on the long run.
It is shown at E on line E A.   In Fig. 69 all the work
is shown in one diagram very plainly, yet to many it
may appear somewhat complicated.   Two pitches in
one roof always make a complication of bevels, often
requiring many lines to illustrate.   As a proof of
the correctness of this method observe the following
point :   A F, A H and J K each represent the hip
rafter, showing it in different positions, and if the
work is right these lines must be of the same length.
A F is the position of the hip for finding the cuts,
while A H is the position of the hip for finding the
bevel for the back of the jack on the short run.   J K
is the position for finding the bevel for back of jack
on the long run.   Having shown the most practical
system of hip roof framing, let us now consider its
application to some of the most complicated plans
which frequently come up in actual practice.

HIPS ON END OF BUILDING OUT OF SQUARE.

A plan of a hip roof with one end out of square is
shown in Fig. 70.   Let A B C D represent the plates
in the plan ; D E C the angle and run of hips on the
square end of the plan, and A F B the angle and run
of hips on the end which is out of square.   In order
to determine the point F so that the ridge of the roof

will be level, make A F II equal to D E G in the plan. From F on line A F square up the rise of hip to I, which connect with A for the hip rafter. Then I is the down and A the bottom bevels. The hip rafters on the square end of the plan will be the same length as A I and will have the same bevels. From F, on the line B F, square up the rise of roof to

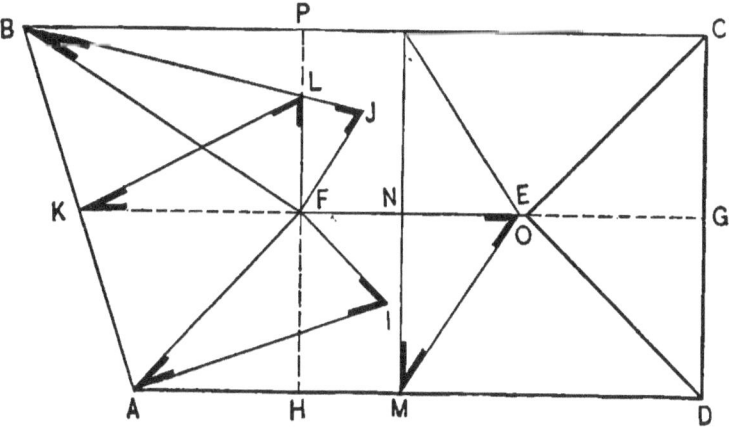

F g. 70.—Plan of Hip Roof with One End out of Square.

J, which connect with B for the length of the hip on the long corner. Then J is the down and B the bottom bevel. K F is the run, F L the rise and K L the length of the common rafter on the end of plan which is out of square. L is the down bevel and K the bottom bevel. M N O shows the rise, run and length of the common rafter on the main plan, O being the down bevel and M the bottom bevel.

To avoid the great confusion of cross lines which would now follow if the work was further developed in Fig. 70, we will dispense with this plan, only taking from it measurements to develop the new lines and bevels of the rafters. Referring now to Fig. 71, let A D represent the plate, A H the run of the common rafter and H I the length of the common rafter on the main roof, which is the same as M O of Fig. 70. Connect I with A for the position of the hip for finding the lengths and bevels of jacks on the front side of plan. Space the rafters on the line A D and draw them perpendicular to the hip.

A bevel set in the angle where they join the hip

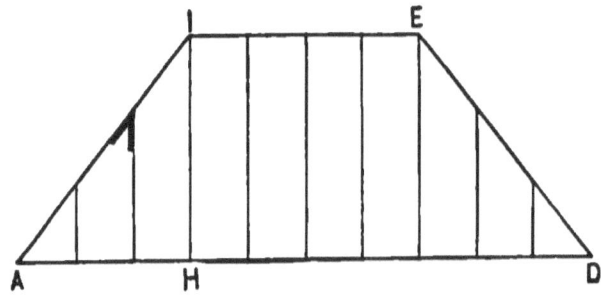

Fig. 71.—Diagram for Finding Lengths and Bevels of Jacks on Front Side of Plan, Fig. 70.

line will give the bevel across the back of the jacks, the down bevel being the same as that of the common rafter on the main part. It is shown at O in Fig. 70. The lengths and bevels of the jacks on the square end of the plan will be the same as the part of the roof already illustrated. The hip rafter D E is the same as A I. We will now consider the end of the plan which is out of square. Referring to Fig. 72, the lines B C A show how much the plan is out of square. A B is the plate, K L the length of the common rafter on the end of plan, being the same as

K L of Fig. 70 ; B L the hip on the long corner, being the same as B J of Fig. 70, while A L is the hip
on the short corner, and is the same as A I of Fig.
70. Space the jacks on the line B A and draw
them perpendicular, joining B A with the hip lines
B L A, which gives the
lengths of jacks on this
end of the plan. The
bevel at E is the bevel
across the back joining
the long hip. The bevel
at F is the bevel across
the back joining the short
hip. The down bevel is
the same as that of the
common rafter shown at
L in Fig. 70. We have
now to find the lengths
and bevels of the jacks

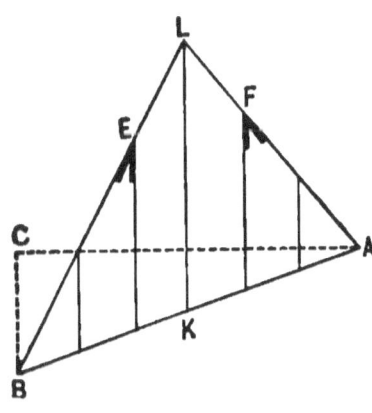

Fig. 72.—Diagram of End of Plan
Out of Square.

on the rear side of the long hip.   Referring to Fig.
73, B C represents the rear plate, B D is the square
of the hip, being the same as B P of Fig 70; D L the
length of the common rafter, being the same as O M
of Fig. 70, while B L is the position of the hip for
finding the lengths and bevels of jacks on the rear
side of the long hip, and is of the same length as
B L of Fig. 72.   The jacks are spaced wider on B D,
Fig. 73, than on B K, Fig. 72, in order that they may
meet opposite on the hip B L.   Draw the jacks perpendicular from B D, Fig. 73, joining the hip B L,
which will give their lengths. A bevel set in the angle
at E where they join the hip will give the bevel across
the back.   The down bevel will be the same as that

of the common rafter on the main part or this side
of the roof.

GABLES OF DIFFERENT PITCHES.

In Fig. 74 is represented a plan of a roof having three
gables of varying pitches. The right gable A B C is
16 feet wide and has a rise of 8 feet. The front
gable D F G is 18 feet wide and has a rise of 8 feet.
The last gable J I H is 21 feet wide and has a rise of
8 feet. It will be noticed that the left gable has two
different pitches. This plan shows as much irregu-

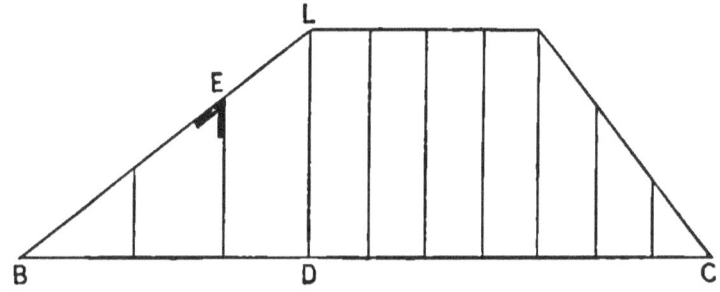

Fig. 73.—Diagram for Finding the Lengths and Bevels of the
Jacks on the Rear Side of the Long Hip.

larity as can be desired and as much as is generally
encountered in actual practice. We will now proceed
to find the lengths and different cuts of the various
rafters required in this roof. The dotted lines represent lines plumb under the ridge of the gables. The
lengths of the common rafters and their proper cuts
may be taken from each of the three gables separately, and are so plain and easily understood from
the diagram that further explanation is unnecessary.
The roof has two valleys of different pitches, of which
the lines N L K are the seats or runs. To find the

length of the valley rafter on the right side of the front gable on the line K L, square up the rise of the roof from L to M, connect M with K, and we have the length of the valley rafter. A bevel set in the angle at M will give the down bevel at the top and the angle at K the bottom cut fitting the plate. To find the length of the valley rafter on the left side of the front gable on the line N L, square up the rise of the roof from L to O and connect O with N for the

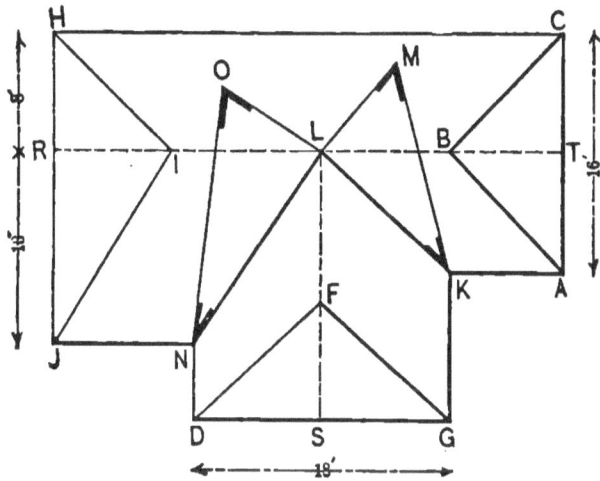

Fig. 74.—Plan of Roof having Three Gables of Varying Pitches.

length of the valley rafter. A bevel set in the angle at O will give the down bevel at the top and the angle at N the bottom cut fitting the plate. Now, if we were to draw all the lines in Fig. 74 necessary to show the lengths and proper cuts of all the different jack rafters required in this roof, there would be such a number crossing each other at various angles as to cause confusion. In this roof there are four different cuts of jack rafters, and it is better not to have them

mixed up with the valleys and common rafters, hence
we will make separate diagrams.

Referring now to Fig. 75, to find the lengths and
bevels of jacks on the front side of right and left
gables, draw a horizontal line, J A, representing the
entire length of front plate line. Next set off the exact location of the front gable N K. From the center of the front gable draw a perpendicular line, S O,
the length of the common rafter on the front side of

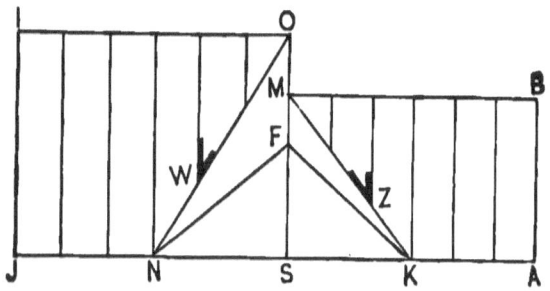

Fig. 75.—Finding Lengths and Bevels of Jack Rafters on the
Front Side of Right and Left Gables Shown in Fig. 74.

the left gable, the same as J I in Fig. 74. Connect
O with N for the position of the valley rafter for
finding the lengths and bevels of jacks on the front
side of the left gable. Square up the length of the
common rafter on the front side of the left gable J I
and connect I O for the ridge line. Space the rafters
on the ridge line and draw perpendicular lines
to the plate and valley, which will give the lengths of
the jacks on the front side of the left gable. A bevel
set in the angle at W where they join the valley will
give the bevel across the back. The plumb cut or
down bevel will be same as that of the common rafter
on the front side of the left gable. To find the lengths

and bevels of jacks on the front side of right gable, set off the length of common rafter from the center of the front gable S M, which is the same as A B of Fig. 74. Connect M with K for the position of the valley rafter for finding the lengths and bevels of the jacks on the front side of the right gable. Square up the length of the common rafter on the right gable A B and connect B M for the ridge line. Space the jacks on the ridge line and draw perpendicular lines to the plate and valley, which will give the lengths of the jacks on the front side of the right gable. A bevel set in the angle at Z where they join the valley will give the bevel across the back. The plumb cut or down bevel will be the same as that of the common rafter on the right gable. The lines N F K show the length of the common rafter on the front gable.

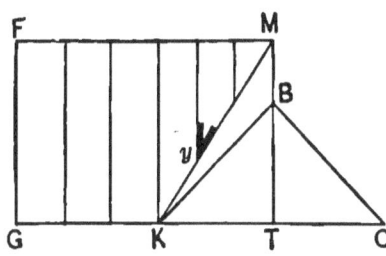

Fig. 76.—Finding Lengths and Bevels of the Jack Rafters on the Right Side of the Front Gable.

To find the lengths and bevels of the jacks on the right side of the front gable draw a horizontal line G C, Fig. 76, representing the plate line. On this line set off the location of the right gable K C. From the center of the gable set off the length of common rafter on the front gable T M, which is the same as G F of Fig. 74. Connect M with K for the position of valley rafter for finding the lengths and bevels of jacks on the right side of the front gable. Square up the length of the common rafter on the

front gable, G F, and connect F M for the ridge line.
Space the jacks on the ridge line and draw perpendicular lines to the plate and valley, which will give
the lengths of the jacks on the right side of the
front gable. A bevel set in the angle at Y will give
the bevel across the back. The plumb cut or down
bevel will be the same as that of the common rafter
on the front gable The lines K B C show the length
of the common rafter on the right gable. To find
the lengths and bevels of the jacks on the left side
of the front gable draw

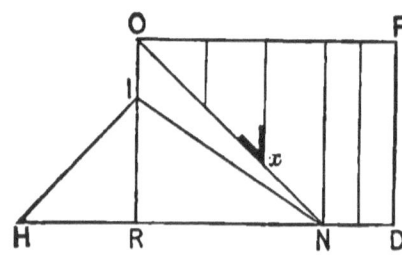

a horizontal line, as H
D of Fig. 77, represent-
ing the plate line. On
this line set off the lo-
cation of the left gable,
H N. From R, the
point directly under
the ridge of this gable,

set off the length of
the common rafter on
the front gable R O,

which is the same as D F of Fig. 74. Connect
O N for the position of the valley for finding
the lengths and bevels of the jacks on the left
side of the front gable. A bevel set in the angle at
.r will give the bevel across the back. The plumb
cut or down bevel will be the same as that of the
common rafter on the front gable. The lines H I J
show the lengths of the common rafters on the left
gable.

In order to throw as much light as possible upon
the subject and present a choice of methods, we will

give another diagram showing the different cuts of
the jack rafters in a much plainer manner, and
which to many, perhaps, will be more satisfactory.
Fig. 78 shows the wall plate lines exactly the same
as in Fig. 74, except it is divided on the ridge line of
the front gable, and spread so far apart that when
the roof is developed, showing the different jack rafters in their various positions, there will not be a

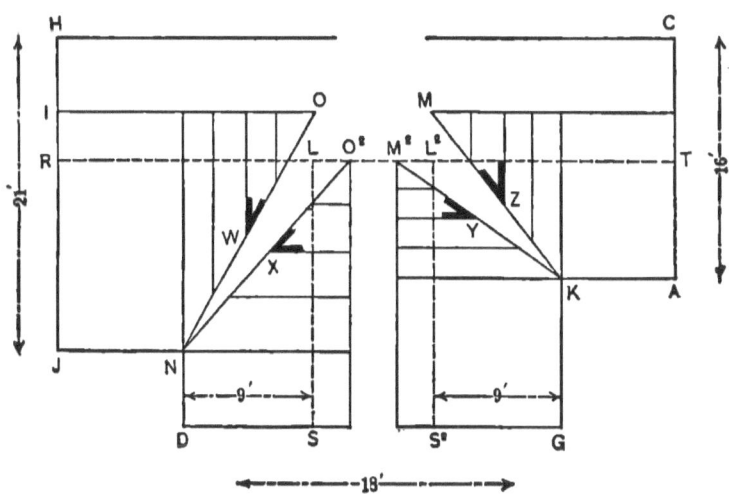

Fig. 7⁹.—Diagram Showing More Clearly the Different Cuts
of Jack Rafters.

series of lines crossing each other to cause confusion.
Let H, C, A, K, G, D, N, J, represent the wall plate
lines. The dotted lines R L S and S² L² T are the
lines plumb under the ridge of the gables. We
will now proceed to find the jack rafters and
their proper cuts : Taking the left gable first on the
line J H, set off the length of the common rafter
from J to I ; from I, at right angles, draw the line
I O, which is the ridge proper and extends to the

center of the front gable represented by the dotted line L S ; connect O with N for the valley rafter ; on the line I O space off the jacks and draw the lines connecting them with the valley N O, as shown in the diagram. This will give the lengths of the jacks in the left gable, and a bevel set in the angle at W will give the bevel across the backs of the same. The down bevel will be the same as that of the common rafter on the front side of the left gable. A similar plan is followed for each gable or each side of a gable, where the jack rafters are of different lengths or have different cuts, as will be readily seen by referring to the diagram. The valley lines N O and N O² are of the same length and show the valley rafters in different positions for finding the lengths and cuts of the two divisions of jacks—namely, the left gable and the left side of the front gable. The valley lines K M and K M² are of the same length, but show the valley rafter in different positions for finding the lengths and cuts of the other two divisions of jacks—namely, the right gable and the right side of the front gable.

Now elevate the four sections of the roof containing the different jacks to their proper pitch, and move the two divisions of the diagram together till the dotted lines L S and L² S² meet plumb under the ridge of the front gable. What is the result ? N O and N O² join as one line and constitute the left valley. K M and K M² also join as one line and constitute the right valley. This would also bring every jack into its required position in the roof, as can be plainly seen in the diagram. The cuts of the two valley rafters must be taken from Fig. 74, as shown and described before. The cuts could be shown in Fig. 78, but as they would only serve to make the diagram more complicated, they are omitted. If any one would like to see a diagram showing all the rafters and different cuts in a roof of this kind, they can draw the lines of Figs. 74 and 78 in one diagram. If they will imagine one of these diagrams placed over the other, the result will probably be satisfactory.

HIP AND VALLEY ROOFS.

In Fig. 79 is represented the plan of a hip and valley roof. This form of a roof is frequently termed broken-back hip and valley, because the main hips are intersected by the common rafters of the gables from one side and the valley rafters from the other. This breaks the line of the hip, hence the origin of the term broken-back. In Fig. 79 let A B, B C, D E and E F represent the line and run of the four main hips. It will be seen that C B is the only hip line which is not broken by a common rafter or a jack from the gables. The main hip line A B is broken at H by the common rafter on the front gable which joins it, as shown by the dotted line G H. If A was the bottom terminus of the hip it would cause several of the common rafters on the left side of the front gable to be cut in two, making more jacks and more work, while weakening the general construction of the roof. In framing, the hip should stop against the ridge of the front gable at H. The hip line D E is broken at I by a jack on the left gable, shown by dotted line I J. In framing, the hip should stop against the ridge of the left gable at I. The hip line F E is broken at K by the intersection of the valley rafter L K. For a scientific job of framing the valley rafter *a b* on the front side of right gable should extend to the ridge of the rear gable, as it is the nearest place of support, and the hip rafter E F should stop at *c* against the valley *a b*. The line B C is the run of the only hip rafter which forms an unbroken line.

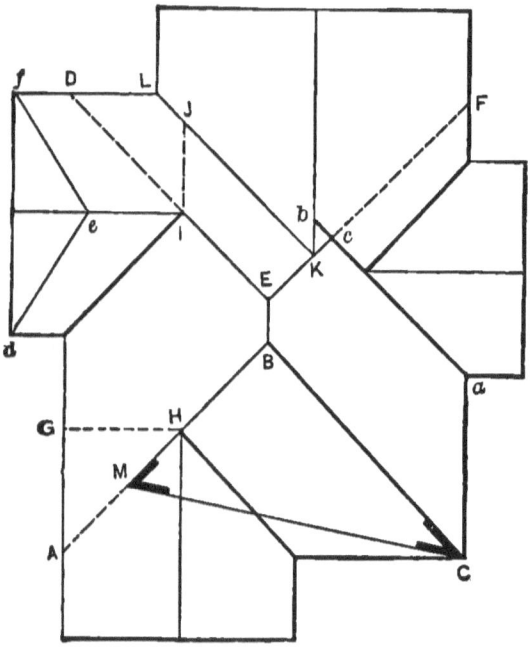

FI, . 79.—P an of Hip and Valley Roof.

From B square down the rise of the hip to M, and connect M with C for the length of the hip rafter. A bevel set at M will give the down bevel and at C the bottom bevel. The method of obtaining the lengths of the hip rafters, which are termed broken back, will be plainly illustrated in other diagrams.

Before proceeding further, however, the reader should be reminded of the fact that on one half pitch roofs the run of a hip or valley is the length of a corresponding common rafter, hence the dotted line D I shows the length of the common rafter on the left gable for a roof of one-half pitch. If the roof was some other pitch—say one-third, for example—then the length of the common rafter for this gable could be shown by setting off the run and rise, as indicated by *d e f.*

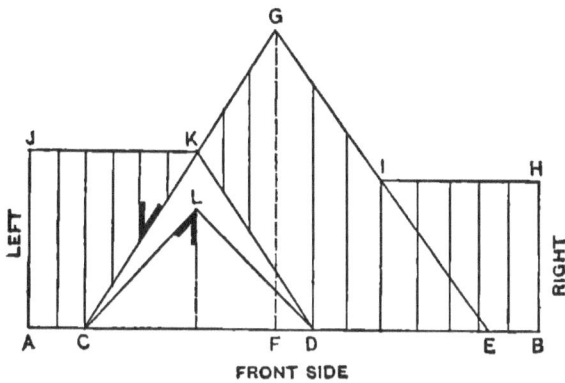

Fig. 80.—Front Elevation of Roof Plan Shown in Fig. 79.

Proceed in like manner with the gables, and also with the main common rafter. Fortunately, there is always an easy way of doing work, and we will now proceed with the method that makes all roof framing easy. Referring to Fig. 80, first draw a horizontal line, A B, representing the front plate, and set off on this line the location or starting points of all hips and gables shown on the front of plan as C D E. Now, C E represents the starting points of two of the main hips, and also the span of the building having the longest common rafter, F being the center of the span. From F set off the length of the common rafter perpendicularly, as shown by the dotted line F G. Connect G with C and E for the length and position of the main hips. Set off the length of the common rafter on the right gable B H, and draw the ridge line H I; then I E is the length and position of the right gable valley rafter. Set off the length of common rafter on the left-hand gable A J and draw the ridge line J K; then K C is the length and position of the left-gable valley. Connect K D for the front-gable valley. Space and draw the rafters as shown, which will give the length and cut of every jack in the front elevation, including those which cut from the broken hip K G to the valley K D. The line K G is also the length of the broken hip, which stops against the ridge of the left gable. A bevel set in any of the angles where the jacks join a hip or valley will give bevel across the back. The plumb cut is the same as that of the common rafter. C L shows the length of the common rafter on the front gable.

In Fig. 81 is shown the right elevation of the roof plan, A B representing the length of plate line, C D E F the starting points of the hips and valleys on the right side of plan, while C and F are the starting points of the main hips. From C and F set off the run of the main common rafter as C N and F O. From N and O set off the length of the main common rafter, as shown by the dotted lines N G and O P. Connect G and P, which is the ridge of the main roof. Connect G C and F P for the main hips. Set off the length of the common rafter on the rear gable B H and draw the ridge line H I. Set off the

length of the common rafter on the front gable A J
and draw the ridge line J K. From the center of
the right gable set off the length of the common
rafter, as shown by the dotted line L M. Draw the
valley from D through the point M, continuing it to
the ridge line or rear gable, which is the nearest place
of support. Then D R is the length of the valley
rafter on the front side of the right gable. Connect
M E for the valley on the back side of the right
gable. C G is the main hip, which is full length.

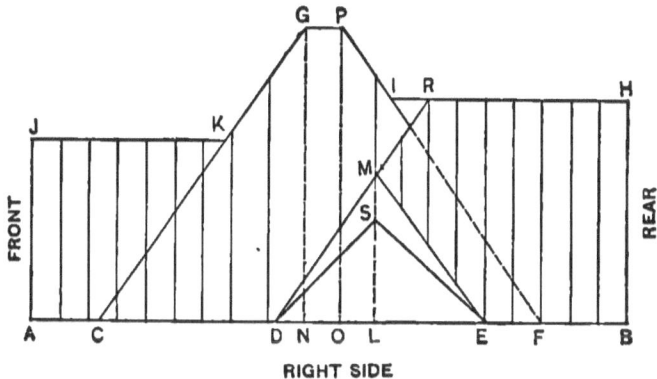

Fig. 61.—Right Elevation of Roof Plan Shown in Fig. 79.

C K is the front gable valley, and the jacks are cut
from the ridge line J K to the valley C K, also from the
plate C D to the main hip C G, and from the ridge
G P to the valley D M. The main hip P F is broken
at I, but extends to the valley rafter D R for a proper
place of support. Jacks are cut from the ridge line
I H and the valley line M R to the valley M E, as
shown. The dotted portion of the hip line P F
shows that if the hip was put in full length it would
necessitate cutting two common rafters and two

jacks on the rear gable, which would make additional
work and have a tendency to weaken the roof.
Thus the length of every rafter in the right elevation
of the plan has been shown, and as the bevels are
the same as indicated in Figs. 79 and 80 further explanation is unnecessary.

In Fig. 82 is shown the left side elevation of the
roof, in which A B represents the length of the plate
line. C D F, the starting points of the hips and
valleys, and C and F the points of the main hips.

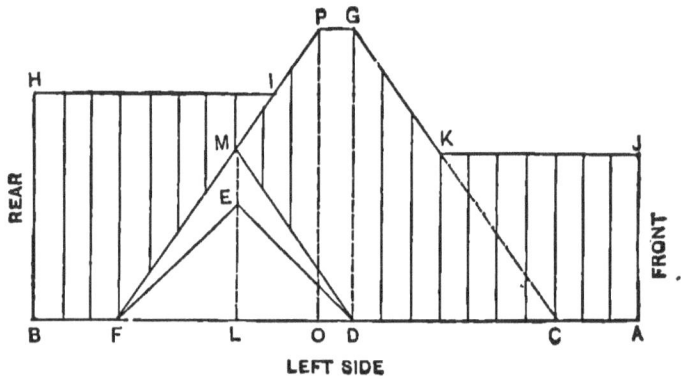

Fig. 82.—Left Side Elevation of Roof.

From C and F set off the run of the main common
rafter, as C D and F O. From O and D set off the
length of main common rafter, as shown by the
dotted lines O P and D G. Connect G and P for the
main ridge. Draw G C and P F for length and
position of main hips. Set off the length of the common rafter on the front gable A J and draw the
ridge line J K. Set off the length of common rafter
on the rear gable B H and draw the ridge line H I.
Now from the center of the left gable set off the

length of the common rafter, as shown by the dotted line L M. Connect M and D for length and position of valley rafter on the front side of the left gable. F I will be the length of the valley on the rear gable. M P is the length of the broken hip which stops against the ridge of the left gable at M, and G K is the length of the broken hip which stops against the ridge of the front gable at K. The jacks are cut from the ridge line H I to the rear gable valley F I ; also from the broken hip M P to the valley M D and from the broken hip G K and ridge line K J to the plate line A D. The length of the common rafter on the left gable is shown by F E. This completes the left side elevation and shows the length of every hip, valley and jack, as viewed from this side of the roof.

The next diagram, Fig. 83, shows the rear eleva- tion of the roof ; A B represents the length of the plate line, C D E the starting points of hips and valleys, and C E the starting points of the main hips. Set off the run of the main common rafter, as E F, and draw the length of the common rafter perpendicular, as shown by dotted line F P. Draw P E and P C for the length and position of the main hips. Set off the length of the common rafter on the left gable, A J, and draw the ridge line J K. Set off the length of the common rafter on the right gable B H, and draw the ridge line H I. From the center of the rear gable set off the length of the common rafter, as shown by the dotted line L M. Connect M and D for the rear gable valley. E G shows the length of the common rafter on the rear gable ; I E is the right gable valley. The broken hip P K stops against the ridge of the left gable at

K, and the broken hip P M stops at the ridge of the rear gable at M. The jacks are cut from the ridge line H I to the valley E I and from the broken hips M P and P K to the rear gable valley M D. This completes the rear elevation and shows the length of every rafter as viewed from this side of the roof. It will be noticed in Fig. 83 that the right gable appears to the left hand in the diagram and the left gable to the right. This is due to the fact that

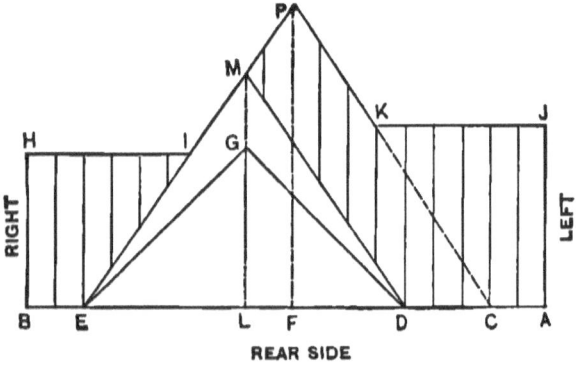

Fig. 83.—Rear Elevation of Roof.

as we view the front elevation of the roof, Fig. 80, we call the gables right and left. Now, if we view the roof from the rear, the right gable will be to our left and the left to our right, as shown in Fig. 83.

AN IMPORTANT POINT.

For the purpose of illustrating an important point in roof framing we will refer to Fig. 84, which represents the plan of a roof having three gables of the same pitch, but the front gable being narrower than the other two. Let A B C D E F G H represent the wall plate and from A set off the run of the com-

mon rafter to I ; square up the rise to J, and connect
A and J for the length of the common rafter on the
main part of the roof. Swing the common rafter
around to a perpendicular position, as shown by A K
on the left gable. Set off the length of the common
rafter on the right gable F L, and connect K with L
for the ridge line. Next, set off the run of the common rafter on the front gable E M ; square up the

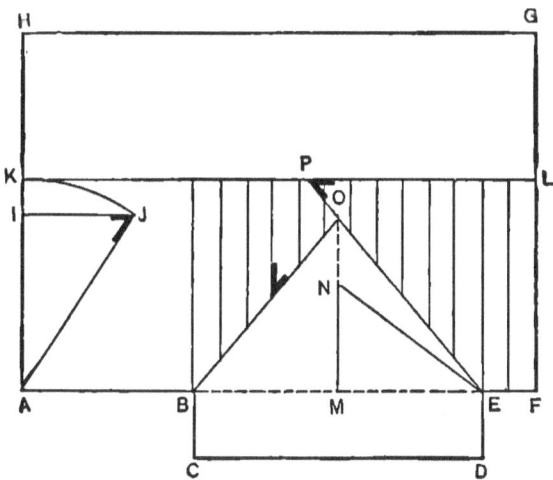

Fig. 84.—Roof Having Three Gables of the same Pitch, the Front
Gable being Narrower than the other Two.

rise M N, and draw E N for the length of the common rafter. From M set off the length of the common rafter perpendicular to O and then draw the
valley from E through the point O, continuing it to
the ridge, which is the nearest place of support in a
self-supporting roof. It is a common practice among
mechanics to stop both valley rafters at O, but this
leaves the valleys without support and as a consequence the roof sags and gets out of shape even before the carpenter has it finished. This is noticeable

on large roofs, where, to secure the greatest strength
in the framing of the roof, it is necessary to run the
first valley rafter to the ridge, as shown by E P, and
butt the second valley rafter against the first, as
shown by B O. E P is the length of the valley rafter
which joins the ridge and the bevel at P is the bevel
across the back of the same. B O is the length of
left valley rafter and cuts square across the back.
The jacks are cut from the ridge to the valleys, as
shown. A bevel set in the angle where they join the
valley will give the bevel across the back. The
plumb cut is the same as that of
the common rafter shown at J. To
find the plumb cut of the valleys
set off the run of the common rafter
on the front gable A B, Fig. 85;
now, at right angles to A B set off
the run of common rafter from B
to C, and draw A C for the run of
the valley. From C square up the
rise of valley to D and draw D A,
which will give the length of the
left valley the same as B O in Fig.
84. The bevel at D, Fig. 85, is the plumb cut and at A
the bottom cut. The plumb cut of the valley E P is
the same as the extension of the rafter to the ridge
line and does not change the cuts.

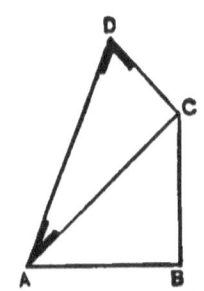

Fig. 85.—Finding the
Plumb Cut of the
Valley Rafters.

OCTAGON HIP AND JACK RAFTERS.

Let us now consider the problem of finding the
lengths and bevels of octagon hips and jacks by the
easy system. Referring to Fig. 86, let A B C D E
and F represent the wall plate line, F G being the

run of common rafter, G H the rise and F H the
length of common rafter.　Next swing the common
rafter round to a perpendicular position, as F I.　Set
off half the side of the octagon A J and square up the
length of the common rafter J K.　Draw K I for the
ridge line and K A for the hip.　Space and draw the
jacks perpendicularly from A J to the hip as shown.
The bevel at R is the bevel across the back and the
plumb cut is the same as that of the common rafter
shown at H.　The length and bevels will be the same

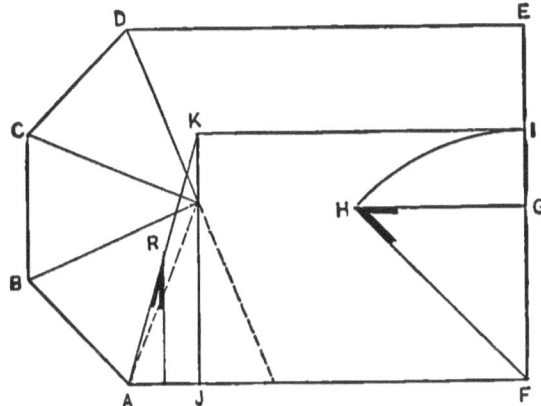

Fig. 86.—Finding the Lengths and Bevels of Hips and Jacks on
an Octagon Roof.

on each side of the octagon, hence further explanation of Fig. 86 is unnecessary.

The cuts of jacks in an octagon, hexagon or a
polygon of any description may be found in the following manner.　Referring to Fig. 87, let A B represent the length of the side, and from the center set
off the length of the common rafter C D.　Draw A D
and B D for the length and position of hips.　Space
the jacks on the line A B and draw perpendicular to

the hips as shown, which will give their lengths. A
bevel set in the angle at E will give the bevel across
the back, the down bevel being the same as that of
the common rafter. Fig. 87 refers only to the length
and bevel of the jacks, but the length and cuts of all
the rafters in any regular polygon may be found in
the following manner :   Referring now to Fig. 88 let
A B C D and E represent four
sides of an octagon. Set off the
center of one side as B F, and
square into the center G F,which
is the run of the common rafter.
Square up the rise G H and
draw F H for the length of the
common rafter. The bevel at H
is the top bevel, and at F the
bottom bevel. G E being the run
of the hip, square up the rise G
I and draw E I for length of
hip rafter. The bevel at I is the
top bevel, and at E the bottom
bevel. From the center of C D

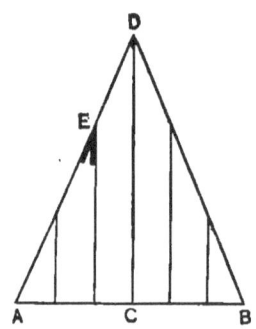

Fig. 87 —Showing how
to find the Lengths
and Bevels of Jack
Rafters in an Octa-
gon, Hexagon or
Polygon.

set off the length of common rafter J K, which should
be the same length as F H.   Draw K C and K D for
the position of the hip rafters for finding the
length and bevel of the jacks. Space the jacks on
the line C D and draw perpendicular to the hips,
as shown, which will give the lengths. The bevel
shown at L is the bevel across the back, the down
bevel being the same as that of the common rafter.

JOINING GABLES DIAGONALLY.

One of the most difficult problems in roof framing
with which the mechanic has to contend—namely, that

of joining a gable cornerways or diagonally to another gable—is illustrated in Fig. 89.   This method is fre- quently adopted in city residences to produce diver- sity in design.   Let A B C D E F G represent the wall plate lines in the plan ; F H, the run of the common rafter on the main part ; H I, the rise, and F I the length of the common rafter. Transfer F I to

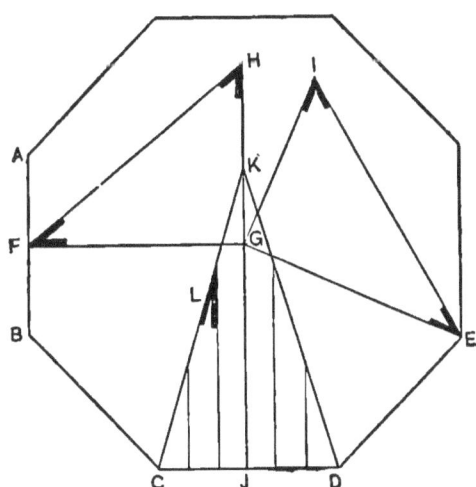

F J and draw J K, which represents the main ridge. From the center of the corner gable square up the rise of the common rafter L M, and draw A M for length of common rafter on the cor- ner gable. From C square up to N what the main common rafter ‹

Fig. 88.—Diagram Illustrating the Method of obtaining the Lengths and Cuts of all the Rafters in any Regular Polygon.

rises in the part of its run represented by L C.   Then L N will be the length of main common rafter up to the point where the left valley starts.   Transfer L N to L O, which is the starting point of the left valley. From O set off O P, which should be the length of the dotted line L G and of the common rafter A M. Square up G R, which should be the same as L O. From R set off the rise of the common rafter on the corner gable to S, which is the same as L M.

From S square up the length of the common

rafter to T, which is the same distance as A M.
Connect T with O for the length and position of the
left valley. Connect T with P for the length and
position of the right valley, which runs from the
ridge of the corner gable to the plate of the corner
gable. Draw P G for the length and position of the
right valley, which runs from the plate of the corner

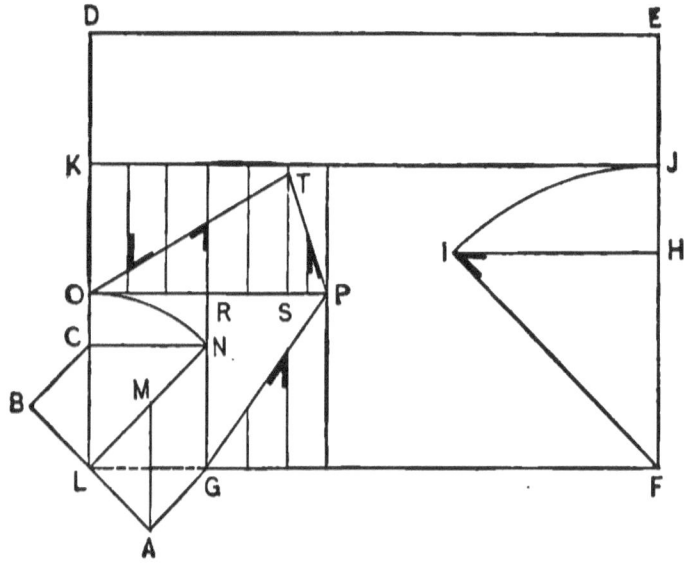

Fig. 89.—Framing Gables which Join Diagonally.

gable to the main plate. Space the jacks on the
main ridge and draw perpendicular lines as shown.
The jacks from K J to valley O T are the jacks in
the main roof. The jacks from O S to the valley O
T are the jacks on the left side of the corner gable.
The valley T P on the right side of corner gable is
but little longer than the common rafter on corner
gable, and runs so nearly straight with the rafters on

the main roof that the jacks on this side are seldom
needed in the corner gable; but in case they are,
space them between S P and draw to the valley T P,
which will give the length and bevel, as shown.
Draw the jacks from the valley G P to the main plate,
which will give the length and cut of the same. The
down bevel of the jacks will be the same as that of
the common rafter.

It is natural for one to think the valley rafter O T

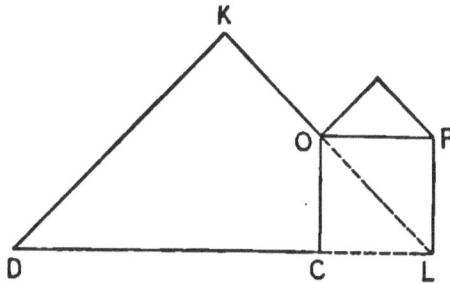

Fig. 90.—Diagram showing Starting Point of Valley between Gables
Joining Diagonally.

should start from the point C, but such is not the
case, as will be plainly seen by referring to Fig. 90,
which shows that the valley starts at O on the line
of the main common rafter, and comes far above the
point C, for C O is the same as C N in Fig. 89.

CURVED OR MOLDED ROOFS.

Having presented to the reader a practical system for almost every conceivable form of straight
work in roof framing, the next step will be to
show an easy system of framing curved, or molded,
roofs, as they are sometimes called. Curved roofs
usually take the form of concave, convex or ogee. An

ogee is a form having a double curve, and is both concave and convex. Fig. 91 shows a conical tower roof,
the rafters being of the concave form. Fig. 92 shows
a convex mansard roof.   Fig. 93 shows an ogee
veranda roof.   These   are   the   principal   forms,

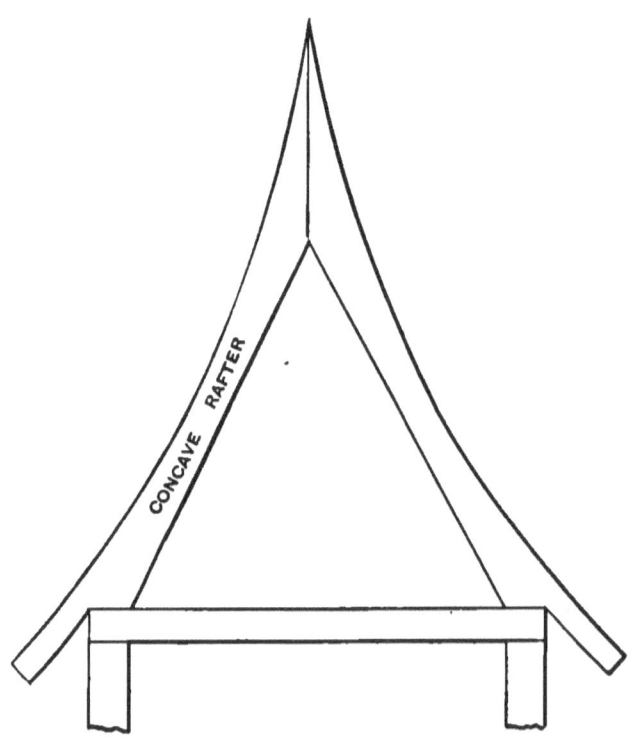

Fig. 91.—Conical Tower Roof with Rafters Concave in Form.

of curved or molded rafters, though they are
variously combined and applied.   The lengths,
bevels and shapes are, however, developed in
much   the   same   manner,   and   when   once   it
is understood how to develop the shape in one form
any shape desired can be readily worked by the

same method. The plan, Fig. 94, represents the corner portion of a roof with ogee rafters. The lines A B and B C represent the wall plates and D E and D F the deck plates. A D is the run of common rafter,

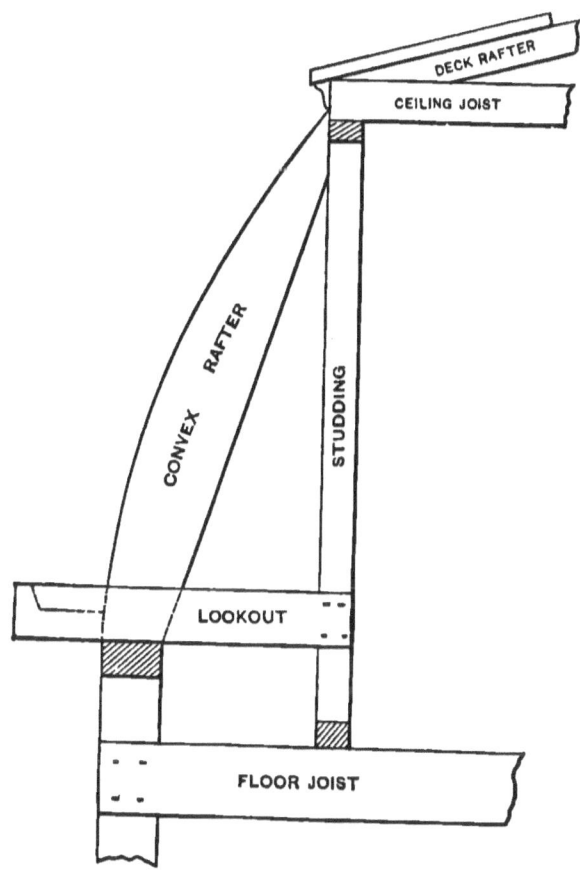

Fig. 92.—A Convex Mansard Roof.

D E the rise, and A E the length of common rafter on the working line. This line governs the pitch of roof and the bevels. E is the down bevel at the top and A the bottom bevel. Connect B D for the run

of the hip, square up the rise, D G, and connect B G
for the length and working line of hip rafter. G is
the down bevel at the top and B the bottom bevel.
To lay out the curved rafter, referring now to Fig
95, set off the run A D, the rise D E, the length and
work line A E. Draw the desired curves, as shown.
H I indicates the bottom edge of the rafter, and J H
shows the width of lumber necessary for making the

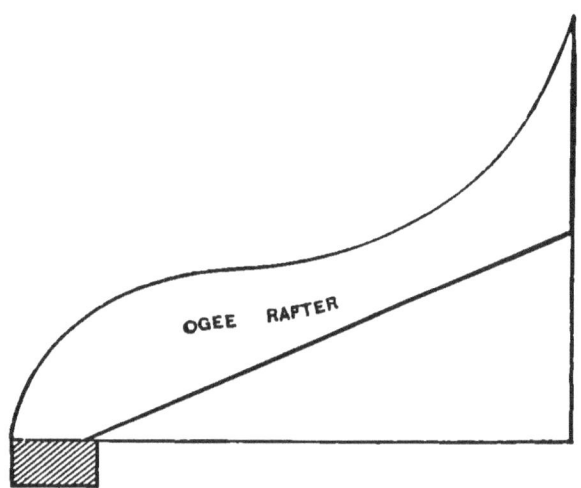

Fig. 93.—An Ogee Veranda Roof.

curved rafter. To economize in the width of lumoer,
the convex portion above the work line may be
worked out separately and nailed on. As a guide in
laying out the corresponding curves in the hip
rafter divide the length of the common rafter on the
work line into any number of equal spaces, as 1, 2, 3,
&c. From these points on the work line square up
or down, as the case may be, to the curve line of the
rafter.

Now we are ready to develop the shape of the hip.

Referring to Fig. 96, set off the run B D, the rise D G, and connect B G for the length and work line of the hip. Divide the work line of the hip into the same number of equal spaces as numbered on the work line of the common rafter 1, 2, 3, &c., and

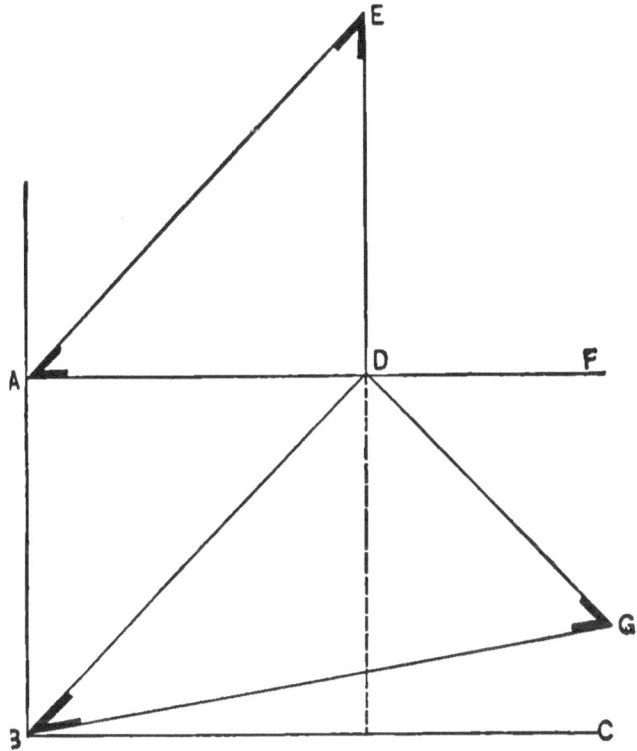

Fig. 94.—Plan of Corner of a Roof with Ogee Rafters.

square up or down, as the case may be, the same distances as shown on the common rafter. Then a line traced from B through these points to G will be the profile of the hip rafter. Fig. 97 represents the corner portion of a roof having two pitches. In this the angle and run of the hip are changed, without changing the method of finding the profiles of the rafters. Take the run, rise and length of common rafter on one side of the hip, and draw the desired shape. Then find the profile of the common rafter on the opposite side of the hip by dividing the work line into the same number of spaces and proceeding as before. The run of the hip being changed, we obtain a different length for the work line. When this is divided into the same number of equal spaces as were the common rafters, and the curved lines traced through the points, we obtain the shape of hip which will correspond to the profiles of the common rafters from either side. In roofs of two pitches it is evident that there must be two sets and two bevels of common and jack rafters. Now in curved roofs the lengths and bev-

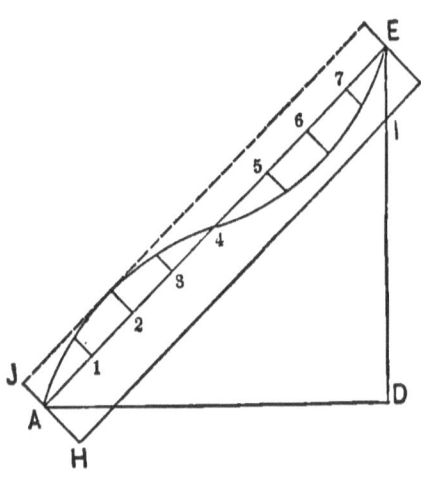

Fig. 95.—Laying out a Curved Rafter.

els may be found by following the work lines of the common rafters, which may be drawn straight, as has been shown in Fig. 95.

The lengths and bevels of the jacks for the different pitches may be found as shown in Figs. 62, 63 or 64. Again, it is evident that a jack rafter must be the same shape as the common rafter on the same side of roof from the bottom, or plate, up to the point where it joins the hip. Hence its length may be found in the following manner by measuring on the work line of the common rafter.

Referring now to Fig. 98, A D is the run of the common rafter, D E the rise and A E the length and work line. To find the length of jack, set off the run of jack A B and square up the rise B C to the work line of the common rafter; then A C is the length of jack on the work line. This method is very simple, yet as it is a new and novel way of finding the length of jack rafters it will be well to point out a common

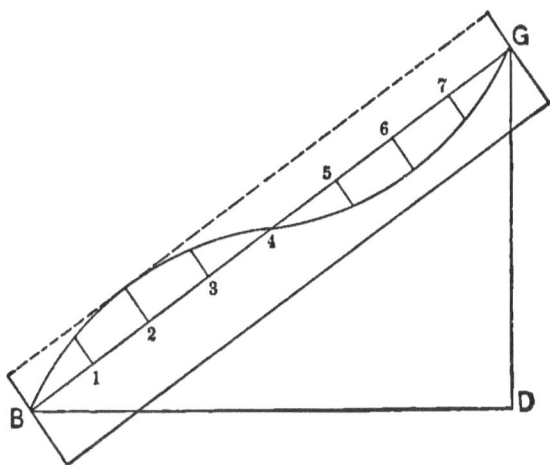

Fig. 96.—Developing the Shape of the Hips.

mistake which the inexperienced might chance to make. Bear in mind that A E is the length of common rafter. B C is not the length of jack, as some might suppose, but the rise of jack ; A C is the length of jack. The down bevel is the same as that of the common rafter. To find the bevel across the back, set off from D the length of common rafter to F, and connect F with A, which shows the work line of the hip. Now continue the line B C to the work line of the hip, and the bevel at G will be the bevel across the top of jack. B G is also the length of jack, and will be found to be the same as A C.

When the bevel of the jacks is known all that is necessary is to square up the rise of each jack from the base line of common rafter A D to the work line A E and take the length from A to the point where the

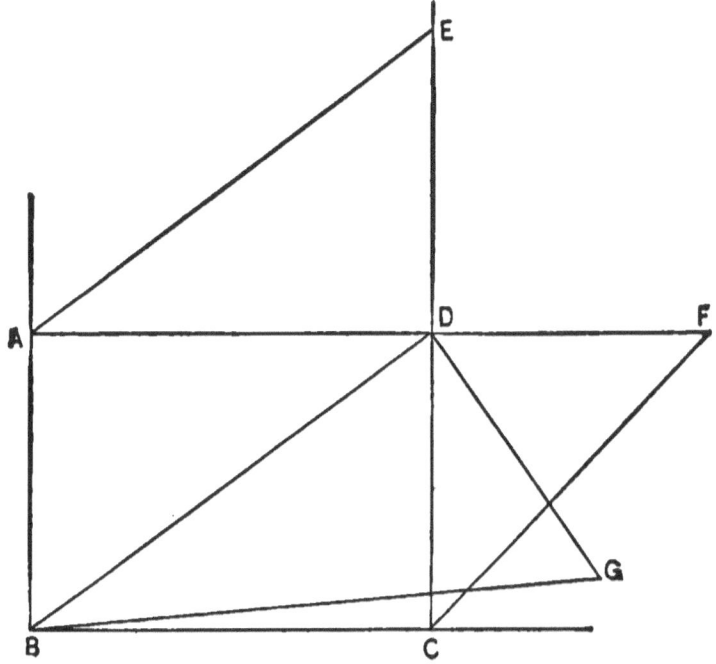

Fig. 97.—Plan of Corner Portion of a Roof having Two Pitches.

rise of each jack joins the work line of common rafter, as shown. Many lines and much time may be saved in finding the bevels of jack rafters on roofs of different pitches by using the plan shown in Fig. 6o, which is the simplest and easiest of all to remember and is applicable to roofs of any pitch,

ROOF FRAMING BY THE STEEL SQUARE.

The lengths and cuts of any rafter, hip, valley or jack on roofs of any pitch may be easily found by a proper application of the steel square and 2-foot rule. There are a few simple facts which, if remembered, will serve to make hip and valley roof framing so plain and easily understood that no one need have any difficulty in finding the length and cut of any rafter. The pitch of a roof is always designated by the number of inches it rises to the foot run, hence the cut of a common rafter is always 12 for the bottom cut and for the top cut is the rise of the roof to the foot. The cut of a corresponding hip or valley of equal pitch is always 17 for the bottom cut and for the top cut the rise of the common rafter to the foot. Thus if 12 and 8 cut the common rafter, 17 and 8 will cut the hip or valley.

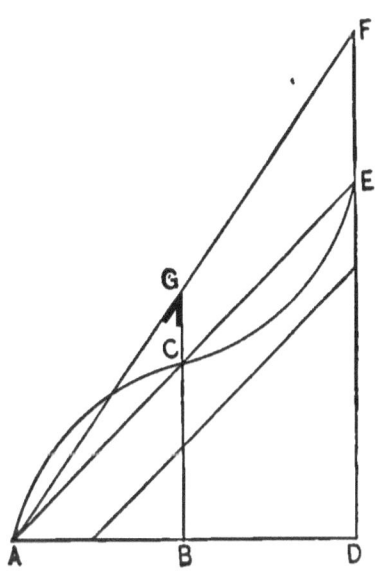

Fig. 98.—Finding Lengths of Jack Rafters.

The top bevel of a jack rafter is always 12 on the tongue of a square and the length of the common rafter for a foot run on the blade. The blade gives the cut. In other words, the run of the common rafter on the tongue and the length on the blade will always give the top bevel of jack rafters on roofs of equal pitch. The plumb cut or down bevel of a jack is always the same as that of the common rafter.

Referring now to Fig. 99, to find the length of a common rafter, take the run on the blade of a square and the rise on the tongue, measure across, and we have the length. For example, if the run of a rafter is 12 feet and the rise 8 feet, take 12 inches on the blade and 8 inches on the tongue and measure across, which will give the length, 14 7-16 inches, equal to 14 feet 5¼ inches, 12 and 8 giving the cuts. The blade

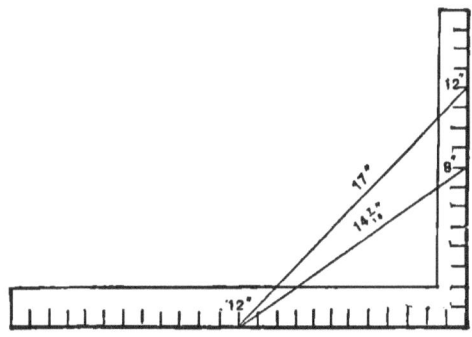

Fig. 99.—Finding Length of a Common Rafter by means of the Steel Square.

gives the bottom cut and the tongue the top cut. To find the length of a corresponding hip or valley, take the run of the common rafter on both blade and tongue and measure across, which will give the run of hip or valley, which is 17 inches. To avoid con·fusion by cross lines, refer now to Fig. 100. Take 17 inches on the blade and the rise, 8 inches, on the tongue and measure across, which gives the length of hip or valley 18 13-16 inches, equal to 18 feet 9¾ inches, 17 and 8 giving the cuts. The blade gives the bottom cut and the tongue the top cut. To find the bevel across the top of jacks, take the length of common rafter, 14 7-16 inches, on the blade and the run, 12 inches, on the tongue, and the distance across also represents the length of hip or valley. This merely changes the position of hip or valley in order to obtain the bevel across the top of jacks, which is 12 on the tongue and 14 7-16 on the blade. The blade gives the cut. The plumb cut or down bevel is the same as that of the common rafter.

The lengths of the jacks may be obtained in the

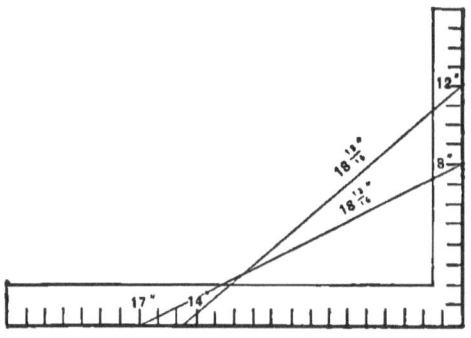

Fig. 100 —Finding Leng'h of Hip or Valley Rafter.

following manner : Take the run of common rafter on the blade, 12 inches, and the length, 14 7-16 inches, on the tongue, and lay a straight edge across, as shown in Fig. 101. Space the jacks on the blade of the square, which represents the run of common rafter, and measure perpendicularly from the tongue to the straight edge on the line of each jack for their length.

The lengths of hips, valleys and jacks on roofs of unequal pitches may be found in the same manner by taking figures on the blade and tongue of a

square which will represent the different pitches.
For example, suppose a roof hips 9 feet on the right
side of the hip and 13 feet on the left and has a rise
of 8 feet, what will be the lengths and bevels of the
rafters? Referring to Fig. 102, take 13 inches on the
blade of a square and 8 inches on the tongue and
measure across. This gives 15¼ inches, equal to 15
feet 3 inches, which is the length of the common
rafter on the left side of hip. Now, 13 inches on the

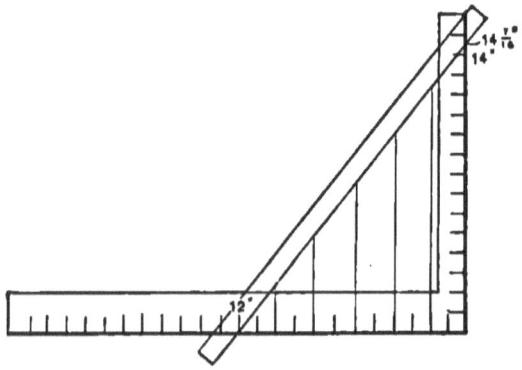

Fig. 101.—Obtaining the Lengths of Jack Rafters with the
Steel Square.

blade and 8 inches on the tongue give the cuts, the
tongue giving the top cut and the blade the bottom
cut fitting the plate. Now take the length of common rafter on the left side, 15¼ inches, on the blade,
and the run of the common rafter on the right side
of hip, 9 inches, on the tongue and the blade will give
the cut across the back of the jack rafters on the left
side of the hip. The lengths of the jacks may be
found in the following manner: Divide the length of
common rafter by the number of spaces for jacks.
This will give the length of the shortest jack and the

second will be twice that length, the third three
times, and so on till the required number are found.
Each side of the hip may be worked in the same
manner till all the different lengths and cuts are
found. The whole thing boiled down results in a
few simple facts : 1, that the run of the common
rafter on the tongue of a square and the length of
the common rafter on the blade will always give
the bevel across the back of a jack rafter on roofs
of equal pitch ; 2, if the roofs are of different

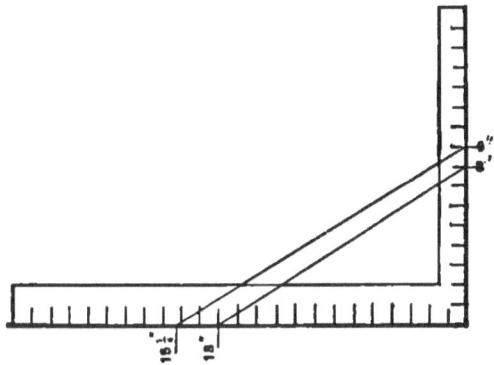

Fig. 102.—Finding Lengths and Bevels of
Rafters on Roofs of Unequal Pitches.

pitches the length of the common rafter on the blade
and the run of the common rafter on the opposite
side of the hip or valley on the tongue will give the
cut of the jack on the side of the roof from which
the length of the common rafter was taken. The
blade gives the cut. Hence the bevels of jack
rafters on roofs of different pitches may be found as
easily as on roofs of equal pitch.

The next step will be to show a simple plan for obtaining the length and cuts of the hip rafter by

means of the square and 2-foot rule. As the run of common rafter on the left side of hip is 13 inches and on the right side 9 inches, we will take figures on the blade and tongue of a square which will represent the runs of the common rafters. Referring to Fig. 103, take 13 inches on the blade and 9 inches on the tongue and measure across and we have 15 10-12 inches, equal to 15 feet 10 inches, the run of the hip rafter. Now take the run of the hip, 15 10-12 inches, on the

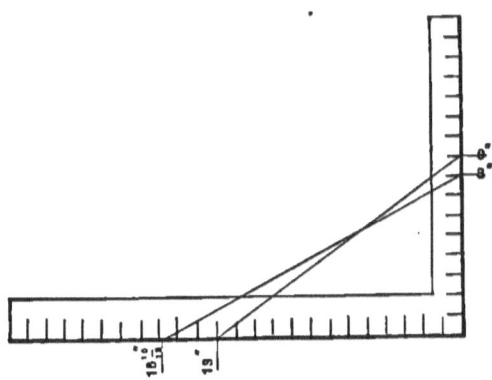

Fig. 103.—Obtaining Length and Cuts of Hip Rafter by means of Steel Square and Two-Foot Rule.

blade and the rise of the roof, 8 inches, on the tongue, and measure across and we have the length of the hip rafter, 17¾ inches, equal to 17 feet 9 inches. Now, 8 inches on the tongue and 15 10-12 on the blade will give the cuts. The tongue gives the down bevel at the top and the blade the bottom cut fitting the plate.

ROOF FRAMING WITHOUT DRAWINGS.

The system to which we shall now refer is one by which the lengths of common rafters, hips, valleys and jacks, with all their different bevels, on roofs of equal pitch, may be easily found without the aid of drawings. It is so simple that any one can understand it and find the lengths and cuts in less time than it takes to describe the operation. The system consists of a table, given below, from which the lengths and cuts of any rafter may be determined at once :

Rafter Table.

1	2	3	4	5	6
Pitch of roofs.	Common rafter, 1 foot run.	Corresponding hips or valleys.	Common rafter cuts.	Hip and valley rafter cuts.	Jack rafter cuts.
Inches.	Feet.	Feet.	Inches.	Inches.	Inches.
6	1.12	1.50	12 and 6	17 and 6	13½ and 12
7	1.16	1.53	12 and 7	17 and 7	13⅝ and 12
8	1.20	1.56	12 and 8	17 and 8	14⅜ and 12
9	1.25	1.60	12 and 9	17 and 9	15 and 12
10	1.30	1.64	12 and 10	17 and 10	15⅝ and 12
12	1.42	1.73	12 and 12	17 and 12	17 and 12
15	1.60	1.88	12 and 15	17 and 15	19¼ and 12
18	1.80	2.07	12 and 18	17 and 18	21⅝ and 12

Column 1 shows the pitch of roofs in the number of inches rise to the foot run. Column 2 shows the length of common rafter to a foot run. Column 3 shows the length of a hip or valley corresponding to a foot run of the common rafter. Column 4 shows the figures to take on the square for the top and bottom cuts of the common rafter—namely, 12 for the bottom cut, and for the top cut the number of inches the common rafter rises to the foot run. Column 5 shows what figures to take on the square for the top and bottom cuts of a corresponding hip or valley, which is always 17 for the bottom cut and the number of inches the common rafter rises to the foot run for the top cut. Column 6 shows what figures to take on the square for the top bevel of the jack rafters, which is always 12 on the tongue of a square and the length of the common rafter for a foot run on the blade. The blade gives the cut. The plumb cut or down bevel is always the same as that of the common rafter.

To avoid a complication of fractions the figures given in columns 2 and 3 are in feet and decimals. To find the length of common rafters, hips, valleys and jacks, it is only necessary to multiply the run by the figures given corresponding to the pitch.

We will now give a practical example showing how to find the lengths of rafters by means of the table.

Example.—What will be the length of rafters on a building 16 feet wide, with roof of 7 inches pitch, hipped to the center and rafters placed 16 inches from centers?

Analysis.—The run of the common rafter is one-half the width of the building, which is 8 feet. Multiplying the run by the length of rafter for 1 foot, 7-inch pitch, column 2 of the table, and pointing off the product as in multiplication of decimals, we have the length of rafter in feet and a decimal of a foot. The decimal must be multiplied by 12 to reduce it to inches.

Operation —1.16 × 8 = 9.28 feet.   0.28 × 12 = 3.36 inches. Thus the length of the common rafter is 9 feet 3.36 inches. The 0.36 is a decimal of an inch, and if great accuracy is desired it may be called ⅜ inch. The table is made to give the length in full, so that very slight decimals may be disregarded altogether. The corresponding hip or valley may be found as follows: 1.53 × 8 = 12.24 feet. 0.24 × 12 = 2.88 inches. The decimal o 88 may be called ⅞ inch. Thus the length of the hip would be 12 feet 2⅞ inches.

If the rafters are placed 16 inches from centers the run of the first jack will be 16 inches. Taking the same figures in the table as those to find the common rafter and multiplying by 16 inches, we have as follows ·

$$1.16 \times 16 = 18.56$$

The decimal 0.56 may be called ½ inch. Thus the length of the first jack would be 18½ inches, the second twice that, the third three times, and so on till the required number is found. In complicated roofs the table may be used to great advantage in connection with the plan. When used in this way only one diagram showing the runs of the rafters is needed, as the lengths of all the rafters may be very quickly figured and set down on the plan and the required bevels may be taken from the table. Fig. 104 shows the plan of a roof 16 x 24 feet, with wing 12 x 8 feet. Roof to be 8 inches to the foot pitch and rafters placed 2 feet from centers. The lengths of rafters in this plan figured by the table are as follows :

For the common rafter, main part,

1.20 × 8 = 9.60 feet.   0.60 x 12 = 7.20 inches.

Length of common rafter is therefore 9 feet 7 inches.

For the hip rafter, main part,

1.56 × 8 = 12.48 feet.   0.48 × 12 = 5 76 inches.

The length of hip rafter is therefore 12 feet 5¾ inches.

For the first jack, main part,

1.20 × 2 = 2.40 feet.   0.40 × 12 = 4.80 inches.

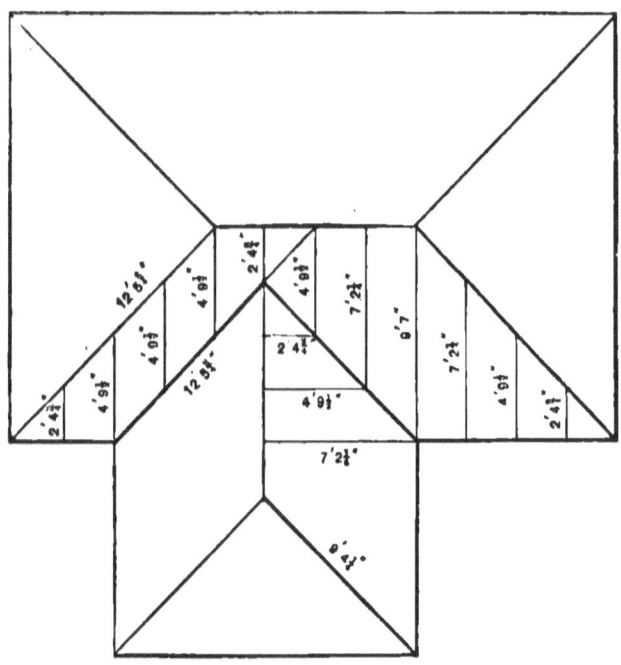

Fig. 104.—Showing how a Plan of a Roof can be used in
Connection with Rafter Table.

The length of first jack is 2 feet 4¾ inches; the length of the second jack is 4 feet 9½ inches, and the length of the third jack is 7 feet 2¼ inches.

For the hip rafter on the wing:

1.56 × 6 = 9.36 feet.   0.36 × 12 = 4.32 inches.

The length of hip rafter is therefore 9 feet 4¼ inches

Thus we have computed the different lengths of all the rafters necessary to figure in the plan, as all rafters of the same run will be the same length, these being readily seen in the plan. As the latter shows the lengths of the principal different rafters it is unnecessary to represent all those which are of the same length, although it is a good plan in actual practice. By this method one can see at a glance just where every rafter belongs, as well as noting instantly all of the same length. It is usually necessary to figure the lengths of only a few, as will be seen by referring to the plan. The valley rafter on the left side of the wing should be the same length as the main hip; then it will reach to the main ridge, the only place of support in a self-supporting roof. The jacks which cut from hip to valley on this side will each be the same length, which is 4 feet 9½ inches, the length of the second jack, as shown in the plan. The valley on the right side of the wing will be the same length as the hip on the end of the wing. The common rafter on the wing will be the same length as the third jack on the main part. It is easy to see that the length of any rafter on roofs of equal pitch may be readily found by this method.

LAYING OUT RAFTERS.

In laying out rafters, it is very important to set off the length on the work line, as deviations from this rule will often lead to mistakes. The lines indicating the run and rise of a rafter are easily traced, but the work line for the length of a rafter is sometimes lost to sight, particularly in cutting jack rafters. The framer must never lose the work line in cutting

a rafter; if he does, he is like a mariner at sea without a compass or a ship without a rudder.   The
work line is an important part in obtaining the
lengths of rafters, as will be shown.

In roofs which have a projection of the rafter for
the cornice, the back of the rafter rises above the
level of the plate whatever thickness may be allowed
on the rafter for the support of the cornice.   Refer-

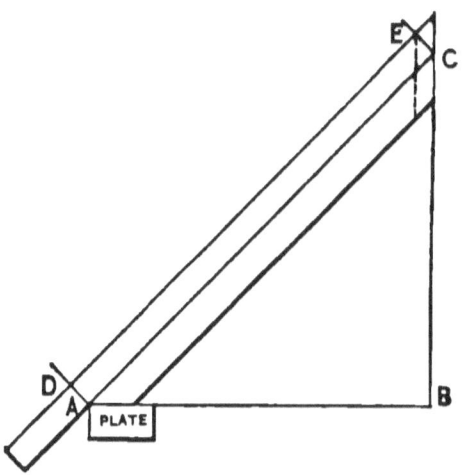

Fig. 105 —Diagram Showing Importance of Work Line in
Laying out Rafters.

ring to Fig. 105, A B represents the run of a common
rafter, B C the rise, and A C the length and work
line.   Projections for the cornice must be added
from the corner of the plate at A.   Now suppose we
square up from the corner of the plate at A to D, the
back of the rafter, and measure the length to E the
same as on the line A C.   Now if we make the plumb
cut at E, as shown by the dotted line, we find our
rafter too short, as is plainly shown in the diagram.

Thus it will be seen that the work line is an essential point in laying out rafters.

We will now trace the work line in a jack rafter from the plate to the top bevel, as this is the place many mechanics are at a loss as to the proper point to which to measure.

Referring to Fig. 106, we can easily trace the work line and the lines forming the cut of the jack rafter. The work line is represented by A C, the plumb line or down bevel by D B', and is always the same as the down bevel of the common rafter. To find the bevel across the back of the rafter draw another plumb line the thickness of the rafter from the cutting line

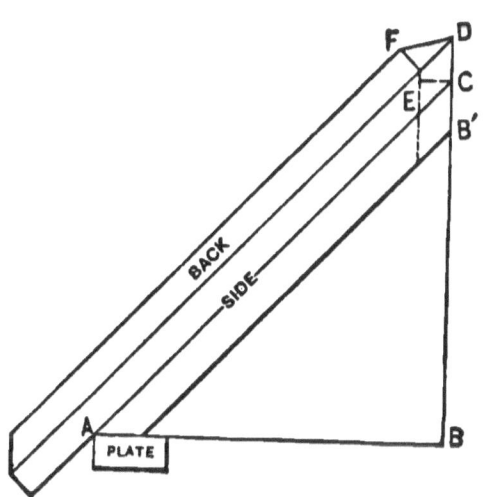

Fig. 106.—Diagram Showing Work Line in a Jack Rafter.

and measured square from it, as C E. Square across the back of the rafter to F ; connect F with D, and the lines to which to cut are F D B'. The proper point to which to measure on the line A C is from A to the scratch mark half way between the two plumb lines, this being the center of the rafter in thickness. In actual practice this little point need not be considered, and for convenience in measuring the length may be taken from A to C. So slight a deviation in

the true length of a jack rafter does not cut any
figure in framing or ever appear noticeable, from the
fact that jack rafters can be moved forward or back-
ward a little on the plate and hip and if they are all
framed by the same rule will be of uniform distance
apart.

We are instructed by some to deduct half the
thickness of the hip or valley rafter in setting off the
length of jacks. This is a point which may be disregarded, especially when hip and valley rafters are
only 2 inches thick.   It is evident that if we lay
out a jack rafter setting off the length on the side
which has the long corner of the bevel, it will be a
little more than half the thickness of the rafter short
when the bevel is cut.

Therefore, if jacks are cut according to the work
line in Fig. 106, they will be near enough for all
practical purposes in the usual order of building and
without making any deduction in length for the
thickness of hip and valley rafters. When roofs have
a ridge pole deduct half its thickness from the
length of the common rafter. Aside from this, it is
seldom necessary to make any reduction in the
lengths of rafters, as shown on the work lines in the
plans.

RAISING RAFTERS.

It is as important to know how to properly put
up the frame work of a roof as it is to know how to
lay it off correctly. First see that the plates are
straight and the angles true, then set up the deck or
ridge on stanchions the proper hight ; next put up
all the common rafters which will not interfere with
hips and valleys. Many mechanics advocate raising

the hips and valleys first, but practical experience will prove that this is a great mistake. Put up first all the common rafters that can be raised conveniently. There is always a ready way to plumb a pair of common rafters, and if the common rafters are plumb they will square up the roof ready for hips and valleys, which, being on an angle with the plates, are often very bothersome to set to the required angle. They are also troublesome to plumb up, especially when they are the first rafters raised. By raising the common rafters first the deck or ridge is brought into the proper position for the hips and valleys and the trouble of squaring and plumbing the hips and valleys is much less. After raising the hips and valleys stay them straight and finally put in the jacks, being careful not to spring the hips and valleys when nailing the jacks.

MITERING PLANCEERS, MOLDINGS, &c.

As the art of making a common miter joint is universally understood by all mechanics, an explanation of the common miter is unnecessary. We will, therefore, explain the methods of making some of the most complicated and difficult miters which frequently come up in the actual practice of carpentry. Fig. 107 shows the elevation of a roof having three gables, and it is required to miter the level planceer A B with the gable planceer B C. To many this seems like a difficult problem ; yet if one will consider the roof plan for a moment, he will see that the proper figures on the square to make the required

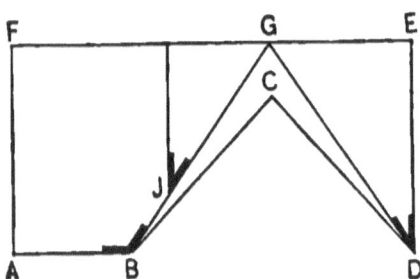

Fig. 107.—Elevation of Roof Having Three Gables.

miter may be taken directly from the roof plan, which gives the bevels for cutting the rafters.

To cut the bevel on the planceer A B use the same figures on the square that make the bevel across the top of jacks, but reverse the cut. Thus, if 17 on blade and 12 on tongue cuts the jack rafters, the blade gives the cut of the jack and the tongue the miter line for the planceer. The reason for reversing the cut is because the planceer A B runs in a direction exactly opposite the rafters.

The same figures will also miter the sheeting in the valley. Now, the planceer B C which goes up the gable runs parallel with the rafters, hence the same figures which give the cut for the jacks will give the cut for this, which, in the present case, are 17 on the blade and 12 on the tongue, the blade giving the cut. Or, referring to Fig. 107, B G and D G show the position and length of valley rafters, and the bevel at B is the bevel for cutting the planceer A B, while that at J, which is the bevel for jack rafter, is the bevel for cutting the planceer B C, which goes up the gable. The junction of the two gable planceers C D and E D at D forms another kind of miter joint. In this the planceer on both gables cuts the same, and the cut is the same as the bevel which cuts the jacks, shown at D. This bevel is also the same as the one shown at J.

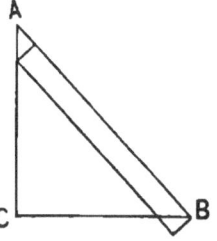

Fig. 108.—Diagram for Finding Width of Gable Planceer.

The planceers A B and B C must necessarily be of different widths, the gable planceer being the narrower. To find the width the gable planceer must be to match the level planceer, draw the width of level planceer A B, representing the pitch of roof, as shown in Fig. 108. Square down from A to C, the rise of planceer, and B C will be the width of gable planceer corresponding to A B. To obtain the miter line for mitering the fascia and crown molding at B, draw two parallel level lines and two parallel pitch lines of the common rafter, keeping both sets of lines the same distance apart, as shown in Fig. 109. Connect the opposite angles where the

lines cross each other, as shown by A B, and this will
give the required miter. The figures for this may be
found by placing the blade of the square on the line
A C and tongue on A B. The tongue gives the cut
If the fascia stands square with the rafters on the
line A B, Fig. 107, then a square miter will make the
joint which connects the level fascia A B with the
gable fascia A F. But now suppose the fascia on
line A B stands plumb, as it frequently does, and
should on a roof of this kind, then a different cut is
required. In this case cut the level fascia on a
square miter, but for
the gable fascia cut
across the edge of
the board on the
same bevel as for a
jack, and cut the
plumb line the same
as that of the com-
mon rafter.

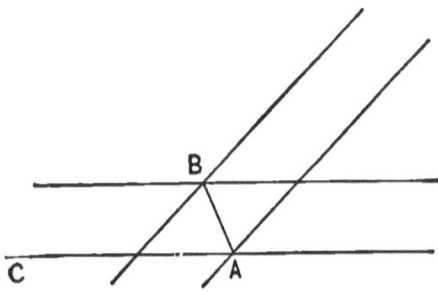

Fig. 109.—Method of Obtaining Miter Line
for Fascia and Crown Molding.

Having shown
how to properly miter the planceer and fascia,
we will next take the crown molding. The miter
for moldings cannot be accurately laid off from
the square because it cannot be properly applied
to them; hence the best way to miter moldings
is by means of the miter box. As almost every one
knows how to make the common miter box I
will not go into the details of manufacturing it,
but explain the methods of making cuts in it for
the purpose of mitering moldings for some of the
difficult joints which frequently come up in actual
practice.

To miter the molding in the valley at D, Fig.
107, which is the junction of two gables, take for
the cut down the sides of the box the plumb cut of
the common rafter, which in this case I will sup·
pose to be one-half pitch, which is in accordance
with the diagrams. For the cut across the top of
box use the same bevel as for cutting the jacks,
which is shown at J. Fig. 110 shows the manner
of applying the square to the box for laying off

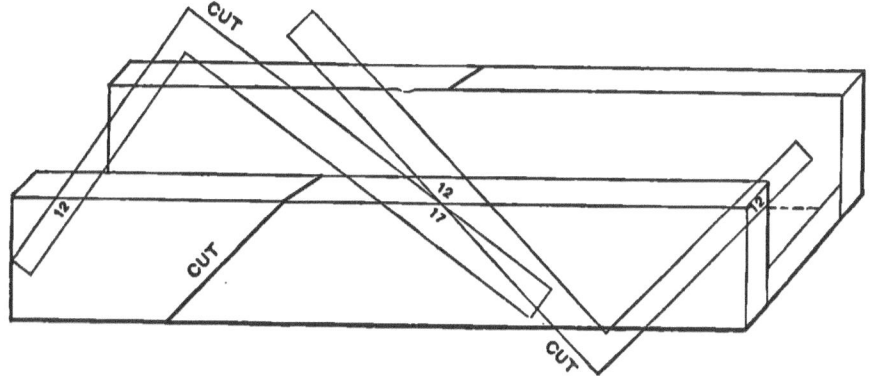

Fig 110.—Manner of Applying the Square to the Miter Box for Laying
Off the Cuts.

the cuts. It will be necessary to put two cuts in
the box, right and left, as shown. In connection
with this kind of a box it is more convenient to
make it with only one side, as shown in Fig. 111.
The side, however, should be made of a thick piece
of lumber, so that it will form a good guide for
the saw. As these miter boxes are used only for
a special purpose no one wants to spend very much
time making them, therefore the box with one side
is recommended to answer the purpose, and it is

the easiest to make. The secret of a good miter
box lies in having the sides stand square with the
bottom and of the same hight from end to end
If these two points are carefully observed and the
cuts made true, good results will follow, no matter
how rough the box may be in appearance.

To miter the level molding at A, in Fig. 107, with
the gable molding A F, cut the level molding A B in
a common miter box, using the square mit r, and cut
the gable molding A F in the box as described in
connection with Fig. 110. By this method a fair job

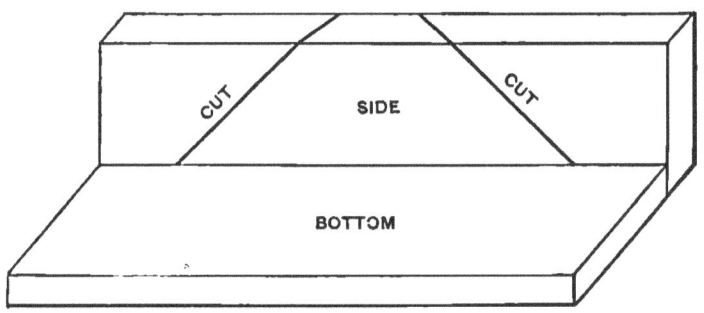

Fig. 111.—Miter Box with One Side.

can be done, but the moldings will not member
exactly. To make a perfect joint the gable molding
requires a slightly different profile.

Fig. 112 shows the elevation plan of a hip and valley
roof drawn to the scale of a third pitch, in which is
shown another form of miter joints. A B is the length
and position of left end hip rafter, C D the length of
common rafter, C E the length and position of left
valley rafter, F G the length and position of left hip
on front end, and F H the length of common rafter.
A B, C E and F G show the miter lines of hips and
valleys. There is nothing peculiar or difficult about

the joints at A, C and E except the mitering of the fascia and crown molding on a square cornice, which means that the ends of the rafters are cut square and that the fascia and crown molding stand square with the roof instead of plumb. To miter the sheeting or the planceer on the hips or in the valley, take the length of common rafter C D on the blade and the run of common rafter D E on the tongue. The figures for a third pitch are 14½ inches on blade and 12 inches on tongue, the tongue giving the cut,

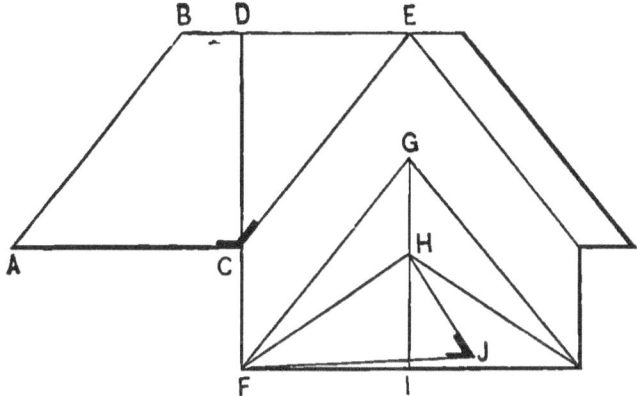

Fig. 112.--Hip and Valley Roof of One-Third Pitch.

or the bevel may be taken at C, as shown in the diagram. There is also a bevel across the edge of the board, which may be found in the following manner : Take the length of common rafter F H on the blade and the rise of common rafter I H on the tongue. The figures for a third pitch are 14½ inches on blade and 8 inches on tongue, the tongue giving the cut, or the bevel may be found as follows : Square down on the line F H the rise of common rafter H J and connect J F. The bevel at J will be the bevel for the edge of the board.

There is practically no difference between a hip and valley cut. The bevel on the edge of board in the valley and on the hip is the same, it being only neces sary to reverse the bevel, as the long point of bevel on hip will be on the face side of board and in the valley it will be on the back side.

To miter the fascia at A, C or F when it stands square with the roof proceed as follows : For the bevel across the edge of board take the length of the common rafter on the blade and the run on the tongue, when the tongue will give the cut. Figures on the square are the same as for cutting the face side of sheeting or planceer, or the bevel may be taken, as shown at C. For the cut down the side of fascia take the length of the common rafter on the blade and the rise of common rafter on tongue, and the tongue will give the cut, or take the bevel shown at J.

To make the cut on a miter box for mitering the molding on the hips and valleys take the bevel at C for the cut across the top of box, which is 14½ inches on blade and 12 inches on tongue. The tongue gives the cut. For the cut down the side of box take the bevel at J, which is 14½ inches on the blade and 8 inches on the tongue. The tongue gives the cut. The facts when condensed are as follows:

Length of common rafter, 14½ inches on blade, and run of common rafter, 12 inches on tongue, gives cut for face of planceer or sheeting. The tongue gives the cut.

Length of common rafter, 14½ inches on blade, and rise of common rafter, 8 inches on tongue, gives cut for edge of planceer or sheeting. The tongue gives the cut.

Length of common rafter, 14½ inches on blade, and run of common rafter, 12 inches on tongue, gives cut for edge of fascia. The tongue gives the cut.

Length of common rafter, 14½ inches on blade, and rise of common rafter, 8 inches on tongue, gives cut for side of fascia. The tongue gives the cut.

MITERING ROOF BOARDS AND PLANCEERS.

To miter planceers and roof boards in valleys of two pitches it is only necessary to take the figures

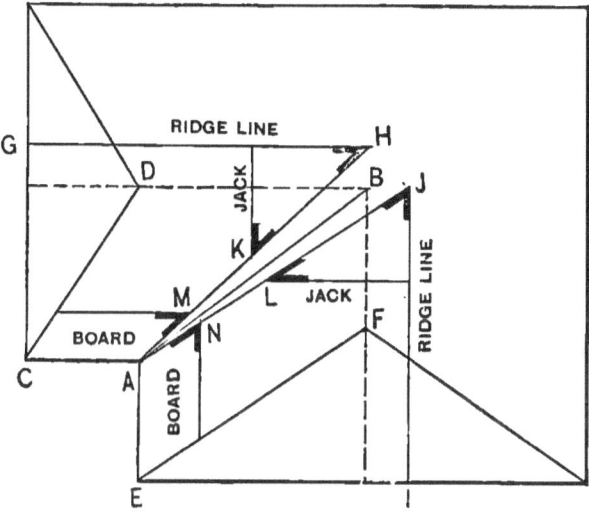

Fig. 113.—Plan of Valley in a Roof of Two Pitches.

on the square which cut the bevels across the top of the jacks on the two pitches and reverse the cut, as the roof boards and planceers run in an opposite direction to the jacks.

The bevels may be taken from any plan showing the two pitches and cuts of jacks. Fig. 113 represents the plan of a valley in a roof of two pitches.

The dotted lines D B and B F are the lines plumb under the ridge. A B shows the run of the valley, C D the length of common rafter on left gable, and E F the length of common rafter on front gable. Transfer the length of common rafter C D to C G and draw the ridge line G H, which extends to the center of front gable. Transfer the length of common rafter E F to E I and draw the ridge line I J, which extends to the center of left gable. Connect A H and A J, which shows the position of valley for finding the bevels of the jacks, roof boards and planceers on both sides of the hip. The bevels at K and L are the jack rafter bevels. The bevels at M and N are the bevels for mitering the roof boards or planceers. The bevels at H and J are also the same as M and N, and show very plainly that they are the reverse of the jack rafter bevels. It is only necessary to have the planceers of a different width in order to have them member exactly, as will be seen by the boards in the diagram. If this plan is followed there will be no twisting of planceers in cornicing when joining roofs of different pitches.

BEVEL FOR HIP OR VALLEY.

A question in roof framing which sometimes comes up in actual practice is how to cut the bevel on the lower end of a hip or valley corresponding to a square cut of the common rafter. This is only used in cutting the ends of hip and valley rafters preparatory to nailing on the fascia and crown molding. Every carpenter knows that a square cut on a hip or valley will not correspond with a square cut on the common rafter.

This cut may be obtained in the following manner:

Take 17 inches on the blade of a square and one half the rise of the common rafter to a foot run on the tongue, and the tongue gives the cut.

For example, suppose I have a roof of one-third pitch. This being a rise of 8 inches to the foot run, 8 and 12 will make the common rafter cuts and 17 and

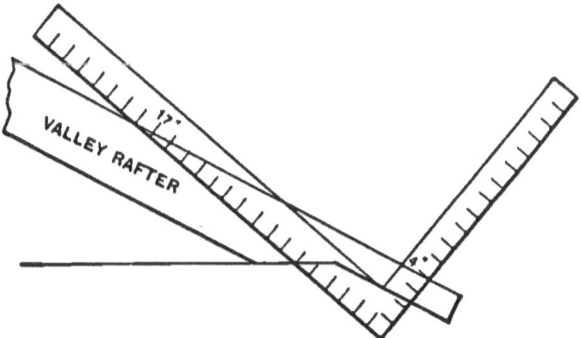

Fig. 114.—Manner of Applying the Steel Square to Obtain Bevel for Hip or Valley Rafter.

4 the cut on the end of the hip or valley corresponding to a square cut of the common rafter. Fig. 114 shows the manner of applying the square for the purpose of obtaining the bevel on the lower end of a hip or valley rafter.

INDEX.